PRAISE

#1 NEW YORK

B

"In the tradition of LaVyrle Spencer, gifted author Barbara Freethy creates an irresistible tale of family secrets, riveting adventure and heart- touching romance."

*-- NYT Bestselling Author **Susan Wiggs***
on Summer Secrets

"This book has it all: heart, community, and characters who will remain with you long after the book has ended. A wonderful story."

*-- NYT Bestselling Author **Debbie Macomber***
on Suddenly One Summer

"Freethy has a gift for creating complex characters."

*-- **Library Journal***

"Barbara Freethy is a master storyteller with a gift for spinning tales about ordinary people in extraordinary situations and drawing readers into their lives."

*-- **Romance Reviews Today***

"Freethy's skillful plotting and gift for creating sympathetic characters will ensure that few dry eyes will be left at the end of the story."

*-- **Publishers Weekly** on The Way Back Home*

"Freethy skillfully keeps the reader on the hook, and her tantalizing and believable tale has it all– romance, adventure, and mystery."

*-- **Booklist** on Summer Secrets*

"Freethy's story-telling ability is top-notch."

*-- **Romantic Times** on Don't Say A Word*

"Powerful, absorbing...sheer hold-your-breath suspense."
-- *NYT Bestselling Author* **Karen Robards**
on Don't Say A Word

"A page-turner that engages your mind while it tugs at your heartstrings...Don't Say A Word has made me a Barbara Freethy fan for life!"
-- *NYT Bestselling Author* **Diane Chamberlain**
on Don't Say a Word

"I love *The Callaways*! Heartwarming romance, intriguing suspense and sexy alpha heroes. What more could you want?"
-- *NYT Bestselling Author* **Bella Andre**

"Once I start reading a Callaway novel, I can't put it down. Fast-paced action, a poignant love story and a tantalizing mystery in every book!"
-- *USA Today Bestselling Author* **Christie Ridgway**

"Barbara manages to weave a perfect romance filled with laughter, love, a lot of heat, and just the right amount of suspense. I highly recommend *SO THIS IS LOVE* to anyone looking for a sexy romance with characters you will love!"
-- **Harlequin Junkie**

"I adore *The Callaways*, a family we'd all love to have. Each new book is a deft combination of emotion, suspense and family dynamics. A remarkable, compelling series!"
-- *USA Today Bestselling Author* **Barbara O'Neal**

"*BETWEEN NOW AND FOREVER* is a beautifully written story. Fans of Barbara's Angel's Bay series will be happy to know the search leads them to Angel's Bay where we get to check in with some old friends."
-- **The Book Momster Blog**

Also By Barbara Freethy

DREAMING OF YOU

Bachelors & Bridesmaids #7

BARBARA FREETHY

HYDE
STREET
—PRESS—

HYDE STREET PRESS
Published by Hyde Street Press
1325 Howard Avenue, #321, Burlingame, California
94010

Printed in the United States of America

Cover design by Damonza.com

ISBN: 978-1-944417-51-2

Chapter One

—➤➤❰❮❰—

Watching two of her best friends, Jessica and Maggie, try on their wedding dresses didn't just bring a tear to Kate Marlow's eye, it also brought home a fairly harsh realization. Once Jessica and Maggie tied the knots at their double wedding in five weeks, she would officially be the last single girl standing—or at least the last single woman in her tight group of college friends, who had made falling in love look remarkably easy the last few years.

"What do you think?" Jessica asked, as she spun around on the dressing room pedestal, looking very much like a princess in the silk and lace dress that was a perfect backdrop for her dark hair and brown eyes. "Is it too much?"

"I was wondering if mine was too much, too," Maggie added, giving her a similarly anxious look, even though the slim-fitting, off-the-shoulders gown, was perfect for her strawberry blonde hair and bright-blue eyes. "I feel like the dress has more lace than I remember."

"And I keep thinking that I already had a first wedding, and maybe I should have gone with something simple," Jessica added.

She smiled at their sudden insecurities. "You are both crazy. Jessica, you look amazing, and your first wedding was at a courthouse in a dress you borrowed from Maggie. You deserve this. And you, Maggie, look like a princess, and what's wrong with that? I like that both dresses are different, unique, perfect for each of you. So, aside from making a few tailoring tweaks, I think we're set, which is good, because the wedding is coming up fast."

She'd never planned a double wedding before, and it was definitely a challenge, especially since the two women were her very close friends. She didn't want to let either of them down or make one feel like she was less important than the other. Their wedding was also taking place on Valentine's Day, which added to the pressure. The most romantic day of the year was busy, and she had to make sure no balls got dropped with the venue, the caterers, the flowers, the band, and all the rest.

"Okay, then," Maggie said, giving her an apologetic smile. "I guess I just need to take the hem up a bit and I'm good to go."

Kate motioned for the seamstress to take that measurement, while Jessica stepped down from her pedestal and walked over to her.

"Sorry for the momentary freak-out," Jessica said, apology in her eyes. "I'm not really the princess bride type."

"Reid is going to lose his mind when he sees you. And you deserve this."

"Thanks for being my cheerleader, as always. Maggie and I really appreciate everything you're doing, Kate. I know we all thought it would be simple and fun to have a double wedding, but I'm beginning to realize we gave you double the work, and it's a busy time of the year. What were we thinking to pick Valentine's Day?"

"You were thinking that it's the most romantic day of the year. You don't need to worry about me. I am loving every minute of this."

"Are you sure?" Jessica gave her a thoughtful look. "You look tired, Kate."

"It's Friday, and it has been a long few weeks. I had two weddings over the New Year's weekend that I'm still recovering from."

"Are you sure that's all it is? I thought I saw some tears in your eyes a minute ago."

"Happy tears. Seeing you both in your bridal gowns made me think about how far we've come from meeting each other our freshman year in the dorms. It's difficult to believe we're all hitting thirty next year. Andrea and Liz both have babies now. Julie is pregnant. And I suspect there will be more children to come. I'm glad we're all still close to each other."

"We made a promise to stand up at each other's weddings a very long time ago. It's your turn to fall in love, Kate."

"I'm too busy to fall in love."

Jessica gave her a knowing smile. "I used to think that, too. I was a single mom with a little boy, a demanding job, difficult parents and an unhelpful ex-husband, and then Reid appeared. He not only rescued me from a doghouse, but from the life I thought I was meant to live. Things can change in an instant—when you meet the right man."

"I know. I'm not worried. My business is booming, and I love what I'm doing. It's all good."

"I'm glad."

Maybe she did get a bit wistful now and then when she saw brides and grooms exchange intimate, tender smiles, but she wasn't going to tell Jessica that. Glancing at her watch, she realized the afternoon had flown by. "Speaking of business, I should get back to the office. Your dress looks perfect, so I don't think you need any alterations."

"I don't. Go, Kate. Maggie and I can finish up on our own. We'll talk next week."

"Perfect." She waved goodbye to Maggie and then headed out the door.

As she left the building, a chilling gust of wind hit her in the face, and she paused on the sidewalk to zip up her coat. This part of San Francisco could suffer some brutal wind coming off the bay, especially in the late afternoon. Thankfully, she didn't have far to go. The bridal boutique was located in the Marina, as was her office, just at the other end of Union Street, about eight blocks away.

As she walked down the popular and busy street filled with boutiques, cafes, bars, and art galleries, she felt incredibly lucky to be living in her favorite city and doing her dream job. Yes, it was crazy, and some of the brides could be very challenging, but it was also fun and exciting and rewarding. She was part of someone's special day and, hopefully, she made their day even more memorable.

Her office was located on the second floor of an old Victorian house that had been converted into two office suites several decades earlier. Charming and romantic, it was the perfect setting for Romantic Affairs, her specialized wedding planning service.

Throwing open the door to her building, she jogged up the steep flight of stairs. There were four rooms on the second floor of the converted Victorian: a reception area in the front, her office, a conference room and a small kitchenette off the back hallway. As she entered the suite, she said, "I know I'm late, but it wasn't my fault."

Shari Jamison calmly raised one eyebrow as Kate hung her coat over a hook on the antique coatrack. Shari was a pretty redhead with green eyes and a very fair complexion. She'd actually been the second bride Kate had ever worked with, and six months after that wedding, Shari had quit her job as a concierge at a downtown hotel and had become Kate's right-hand woman.

"What happened this time—traffic jam, flood or an act of God?" Shari asked dryly, knowing that Kate had a penchant for running late.

"We had to wait for the seamstress to arrive at the boutique and she got stuck behind a broken-down bus and a double-parked truck. Is Melanie here yet?"

"No. She isn't coming. She has a cocktail party to go to tonight, and she decided she didn't have time to squeeze us in. She's going to call and reschedule tomorrow."

She sighed. "This is the third meeting she's canceled. I wonder if she's interviewing other planners."

"Possibly, or she could just be a flake, which seems the most probable explanation."

She pulled the band out of her hair and shook out her long waves, rolling her neck around on her shoulders. "Well, it's fine. I have the Hunts' dinner party to get to tonight. I could use a little break before I put on my happy wedding planner face and try to convince Olivia Hunt to hire us for her daughter's wedding."

"I'm sure you'll be very persuasive."

"Any other calls I should know about?"

"Yes. I spoke to our landlord, or at least a woman calling on behalf of Fox Management, and she said that the downstairs office will be leased starting Monday. We need to move the life-size cupids we accidentally ordered for Davina Smythe's wedding somewhere else before then."

"What?" she asked in dismay. "That's impossible. We'd have to find a storage unit and hire someone to move the dozen six-foot-tall statues. How are we going to do that before Monday?"

"Beats me. She just called. I haven't had a chance to get on the phone and find a solution." Shari gave her a wry smile. "That's a mistake that just keeps on getting worse."

"Tell me about it," she muttered, thinking about the enormous statues that were supposed to have been cute six-inch cupids to go with a floral centerpiece. "I guess we need to figure something out."

"And fast."

A loud crash reverberated through the building. She and Shari both jumped to their feet in alarm. As the sound of swearing drifted up the stairs and through the open door, a terrible thought occurred to her.

"You don't think—" she whispered as the phone rang.

"I think you better go find out. I'll get this."

She hurried into the hall, her mouth dropping

open at the whirlwind of dusty plaster fragments blowing out of the downstairs office. She ran down the stairs, peering nervously into the darkened room for one second before hitting the switch and flooding the room with light.

"What the hell is this? And who the hell are you?" an angry voice demanded.

A very tall, good-looking man stood in the middle of the room, holding a Cupid's arrow in one hand, a layer of white dust covering his obviously expensive suit. "What's going on here?" he added furiously, running one hand through his dark, wavy hair, unaware that he had just streaked it with more dirt.

As he stared dumbly at the Cupid's arrow in his hand, her lips began to twitch at the absurdity of the situation.

"You just got hit by cupid's arrow. You never know when he'll strike," she said lightly.

He stared at her as if she were crazy, and she took an instinctive step backward as he put down the arrow and walked over to her. Wishing she could add a few more inches to her five-foot-three-inch frame, she squared her shoulders and tried not to look intimidated.

"What did you say?" he asked.

"Never mind. I'm sorry. You just looked funny standing there, holding Cupid's arrow." Her voice drifted away. "Can I help you in some way?"

"Yes. You can tell me what the hell these— things—are doing in my office?" He waved one hand around the chaotic room.

Her mouth dropped open in surprise. "Your office? You're the new tenant?"

"I'm not only the new tenant, I'm also the owner

of this building." His voice was clipped and to the point as he began to brush the dust off his sleeves. *His Armani suit was completely ruined,* she thought in dismay.

"I'm Kate Marlow," she said, her humor fading at his words. The last thing she wanted to do was offend the owner of her building. "I own the Romantic Affairs Wedding Agency upstairs, and these cupids are part of a wedding celebration."

"I wasn't aware that you had permission to use this office space."

"Well, not officially, but since the room was empty, the building superintendent said he didn't think anyone would mind."

"He was wrong. And I expect this mess to be cleared out by nine o'clock Monday morning."

"Your office just called a few minutes ago. We'll need a little more time than that. It's already past five now. And it's the weekend."

"That's your problem, Miss Marlow. I have an interior decorator and a contractor meeting me here first thing Monday morning to prepare the office. I don't think I have to remind you that you are not paying rent for this space and are therefore not entitled to its use."

"But what am I going to do with all this?"

"A dumpster would be a good choice."

She flipped her hair back over her shoulder in irritation. "You don't need to be rude, Mr.—"

"Fox—Barrett Fox."

"Right," she muttered. "I'll have these items removed by Monday." She spun around on one high heel and walked hastily out of the room.

"What happened?" Shari asked as she returned to

their suite. "I was just about to come down and rescue you."

"The new downstairs tenant just had a run-in with our cupids, and I do mean run-in. He knocked one or two of them over, and they broke apart, and he ended up covered in dust, holding Cupid's arrow. In fact, it was pointed straight at his heart." She smiled at the memory. "It was kind of funny. Not that he thought so. I'm sure his designer suit will need to be cleaned. We'll probably end up with the bill."

"Probably. So, why are you smiling?" Shari asked with a confused look on her face.

"I don't know. He was just...quite a sight. Oh, and the tenant is also our landlord."

Shari's gaze narrowed. "But this building is owned by Fox Management. They have offices downtown in the Transamerica building."

"That's what I thought, but he said his name is Barrett Fox, and he's the owner."

"Why is he working here?"

"I didn't ask. He wasn't in a chatty mood."

"So, what do you want to do about the statues? I'm heading to Lake Tahoe with Todd tonight."

"I'll make some calls tomorrow. You go to Tahoe and enjoy yourself."

"I hate to leave you with such a big problem."

"Luckily, I don't have a wedding this weekend, so it will be fine. I'm sure I can get them moved into a storage unit. I'll figure it out."

"Then I'm going to head out," Shari said, as she got up and grabbed her purse out of the credenza behind her desk. "Have fun at the party tonight. The Hunts' daughter's wedding could be the wedding of the year, and if we get it, the company bank account will be very happy."

"I'll give it my best shot."

Shari paused at the door. "It sounds quiet downstairs now."

"I'm sure he's gone home to change into another beautiful suit."

"What did you say he looked like?"

"I don't think I said. But aside from the layer of dust, he was tall, dark, and handsome."

"Really? Now I'm intrigued."

"Don't be. He might be attractive, but his personality left a lot to be desired. He was arrogant and demanding and could not for a second see the humor in the situation. I suspect he takes himself very seriously."

"Well, maybe that will change now," Shari said with a sparkle in her eyes.

"Why would that be?"

"Because he got hit by Cupid's arrow. There's a good chance, if that old story is true, that he's going to fall in love with the first woman he saw, and that would be you."

"I'm the last person he would want to fall in love with," she returned, an odd feeling running through her. "And you don't believe in fairy tales, remember?"

"I don't. But you do," Shari said pointedly.

"Well, you don't have to worry. I doubt that arrow came anywhere close to piercing that man's heart...if he even has one."

Chapter Two

An hour later, Kate rolled her neck around on her shoulders, trying to ease the tension out of her tired muscles as her tiny Honda crept along the Golden Gate Bridge, caught up in Friday night commute traffic. After the busy week she'd had, she would much rather be at home in her yoga pants, eating a pizza from Tony's and reading a book or watching a movie. But Olivia Hunt's daughter's wedding could put her company in the black for the year, so she needed to get in a party frame of mind fast.

At least she didn't have a wedding this weekend. She'd have a chance to relax, catch her breath, and, of course, figure out what to do with the cupids.

She smiled to herself as Barrett Fox's image flashed through her head. He'd looked so stunned, bewildered that he'd somehow been attacked by a statue—a statue he probably didn't even understand.

But she doubted he needed to be hit by Cupid's

arrow to find love. Even covered in dust, the man had been impossibly handsome: with thick, wavy hair, a square, purposeful, masculine face, and penetrating green eyes. Those eyes could certainly burn with anger. She wondered what else they could burn with.

Shaking her head at that foolish thought, she focused on the traffic and her upcoming pitch to Olivia Hunt. The woman had invited her to her husband's birthday party, because she'd wanted Kate to see their style and to meet her husband and daughter, Candice, the bride-to-be. She hoped the groom-to-be would also be there, as she liked to meet both the bride and the groom. It was part of her job to be the bridge between opposing styles, which happened fairly frequently between brides and grooms, and with Olivia Hunt in the mix, there would be a strong maternal figure in the plans as well.

While landing the wedding could make her year, sometimes the high-society brides were the most difficult to work with, not that bridezillas didn't come from every economic class.

Traffic sped up as she got to the end of the bridge, and it took only a few more minutes to reach the Sausalito exit. The Hunts' house was located in one of the steep hills overlooking the San Francisco Bay, but the Hunts had a parking valet who grabbed her car at the end of the drive, while another man drove her up to the main house in a golf cart.

The front door was opened by a maid, who took her coat and purse while a waitress offered her a glass of champagne. Very efficient, she thought, her experienced eye taking in the neatly attired help and their quiet, unobtrusive manner. The Hunts obviously worked with party planners and caterers on a regular basis, which made her wonder why they were even talking to her. She knew one of her other brides had recommended her to Olivia, but still…the Hunts could have their pick of full-service firms. It wasn't going to be easy to compete, but she would give it her best shot.

After receiving a glass of champagne, she wandered into the living room, pausing by the bay windows to take in the spectacular view of San Francisco at twilight, the lights on the Bay Bridge, the eerie presence of the hulking Alcatraz prison sitting in the middle of the bay.

Turning away from the windows, she searched the crowd for Olivia Hunt, but it wasn't the bride's mother who caught her eye; it was the tall, dark-haired man in a light-gray Armani suit.

No way!

Barrett Fox was here? What were the odds of that?

Maybe actually not that long. Fox Management was a huge company, and apparently Barrett ran it. Of course he'd know the Hunts. They were all in the same league.

Frowning, she just hoped he wouldn't do anything to mar her chances of winning the job. She hadn't made the best first impression.

She couldn't help noticing that Barrett had not only changed his suit, he'd also changed his attitude. He looked much happier now than he had in her office building. There was a smile on his face as he leaned in to hear what a beautiful brunette had to tell him.

Was that his girlfriend?

Although there was more than one woman in the group surrounding him, so who knew? He was clearly very popular. She didn't notice a ring on his finger. *Did that mean he was single? Or he didn't like jewelry?* Considering the expensive watch on his wrist, she was going to pick single.

But why? He would certainly check off a lot of boxes for most women.

As his gaze moved in her direction, she instinctively tried to hide behind a waiter, but the man moved away to serve canapes to another group, and she found herself looking straight into Barrett's surprised green eyes. A speculative expression spread across his face. He was probably wondering how she fit in to this party of San Francisco elites.

"Miss Marlow?"

She jumped as a woman put a hand on her arm. Turning, she saw the sophisticated and attractive Olivia Hunt, who looked like she was closer to forty than late fifties. Her copper-colored hair was pulled back at her nape, setting off beautiful diamond earrings that sparkled in the light. Her brown eyes were sharp and assessing.

"Mrs. Hunt," she said. "Thank you so much for including me. It's a lovely party."

"I'm so glad you were able to come. Candice will be here soon. She and her fiancé, Anthony, are eager to speak to you."

"And I'm looking forward to meeting them." She paused, knowing she was probably about to be too direct, but it wasn't in her nature not to say what was on her mind. "I appreciate the opportunity to pitch my services. You obviously have a lot of connections with party planners. I'm wondering why you're interested in my small firm."

"Well, as you know, we attended Danielle

Wetherington's wedding last year, and Candice loved everything you did for Danielle. It was beautiful, charming, and personal." Olivia smiled. "My daughter thinks my party planners are more geared to sophisticated and older soirees, which isn't really true, but it is Candice's wedding, and she needs to have a planner she can relate to. I would have been more comfortable using one of my friends, but I'm interested in what you have to offer. Of course, this is just the beginning of several conversations, I'm sure. I'm hoping tonight will give you somewhat of an idea of what kind of party I enjoy."

"I appreciate the opportunity and your candor."

Olivia gave a soft laugh. "And I appreciate yours. Most people don't ask me why I might want to hire them. They're just happy to be in the room."

"I am happy to be in the room and in the running, but I do know that the relationship between the wedding planner and the bride and groom and extended family needs to be in sync. That's when the magic happens."

"Well, that's what we're looking for—magic. Please help yourself to the buffet, mingle, enjoy yourself. When Candice arrives, I'll send her in your direction."

"Thanks." As Olivia moved away, she couldn't help noting that Barrett was no longer in the living room. With any luck, he'd only stopped in to the party for a drink.

She moved into the dining room, noting the glistening china, silver, and crystal, and all the other little party details, so that she could get a sense of what Olivia Hunt liked. Everything was certainly beautiful, impeccable, and very sophisticated.

But what she really needed to know was how Candice's taste differed from her mother's. She was looking forward to hearing from the bride herself.

But as the minutes passed, and there was no sign of Candice or her groom, her party smile began to feel a little forced. It was hard to mingle. Most everyone seemed to know each other, and their circles of conversation felt very closed off. Needing some air, she made her way into the gardens, which offered a patio and fire pit where some younger guests were sitting on couches, sipping champagne and nibbling on appetizers.

The house was built into the hillside, and one garden descended into another. She headed down the stairs to the lowest level, which still offered the same amazing view of the San Francisco city lights. Resting her arms on the railing, she took in a deep breath and let the magical view wash over her. This was the view Candice had grown up with or at least was familiar with. Maybe there was inspiration to be found in the lights.

"Should I run for cover or did you come unarmed?" a voice drawled mockingly from the shadows.

She whirled around at the sound of Barrett's voice. "I thought you'd left the party."

"And I was wondering why you were here," he said, moving into the light.

"Candice Hunt is considering using my services for her wedding."

"Ah, that explains it."

"Why? You don't think I could just be a guest?" she challenged.

"I've been coming to the Hunts' parties for years.

It's always the same crowd. That's why I was surprised to see you—a new face."

"And one you've taken an instant dislike to."

"It's not your face that bothers me."

"Just my statues."

"Yes. Did you make arrangements to move them?"

"I will get them out of there by Monday."

"Is someone really using those statues at their wedding? Are they part of some strange wedding tradition, or just an exercise in bad taste?" he asked, joining her at the railing.

"They were supposed to be six inches, not six feet. They were going to be part of a table centerpiece. But there was a misprint."

"Why didn't you send them back?"

"Because the bride suddenly decided that they'd make a great receiving line for her wedding walk into her reception—like a line of soldier cupids guarding their love."

He shook his head in bemusement. "That's…crazy. I predict that couple will be divorced within two years."

"Why would you say that? You don't even know them."

"No man worth his salt would allow his bride to make a fool of him. That poor guy will suddenly wake up and realize he's been taken for a fool."

"I don't think the groom has a problem with the cupid statues. He also adores his bride and wants to make her happy. Predicting a divorce based on some wedding décor is ridiculous."

He shrugged. "I stand by my prediction."

She frowned at the cynical edge in his voice. "I

assume you're not married."

"Not anymore."

She was surprised. "Oh, I didn't realize…"

"That I'd made it down the aisle? Yes, I did, and that wedding was the most important thing to my fiancée. She spent almost a year planning every last detail, from the swan ice sculptures to the horse-drawn carriage and the rose-petal path to the altar. Unfortunately, it turned out that the wedding was really all she wanted. The marriage could never live up to the hype of that day. We were divorced within fifteen months. All that money her parents spent went down the drain. And it was a lot of money."

"I'm sorry that happened to you." She heard a hint of pain behind the bitter words. "But a big, beautiful wedding doesn't always lead to divorce. Some people get married at the courthouse and don't last out the year. It's about the people, not the party."

"Sometimes. But weddings can get out of hand very easily and people lose track of what's important."

"Well, the brides and grooms I've worked with are very happy in their marriages."

"And how long have you been in business?"

"Four years."

He smiled, as he dug his hands into his pockets. "Let's see where you are in ten."

She frowned at his words. "I think I'll be just fine."

"But will your happy couples still be happy?"

"I hope so. But if they're not, it won't be because of the wedding." She paused. "If you get invited to Candice's wedding, you should say no. No one likes a downer on their special day."

"I'm just a realist."

"I'm a realist and a romantic."

"You can't be both."

"I think I can."

The air bristled between them, but it wasn't so much anger as tension. There was something about this man that made her nervous and irritated and tingly—all at the same time. But she needed to find a way to calm things down. He was her landlord and a fellow tenant. They needed to get along.

"Miss Marlow—Kate?" Candice interrupted, as she moved toward them, a studious-looking man at her side. "I've been looking all over for you. This is my fiancé, Anthony."

"It's nice to meet you, Anthony," she said, relieved by the interruption.

"Barrett," Candice said, surprise on her face, as Barrett stepped into view. "I didn't realize you were here. You haven't come to one of Mother's parties in a long time. How are you?"

"I'm fine."

"You remember Anthony?"

"Yes, of course," he said, shaking the other man's hand. "Congrats on your engagement."

Candice gave her fiancé a quick smile before she said, "We're so excited. We haven't officially set the date, because we haven't picked a venue yet, but it will be sometime next year. We want to make sure that David can be there. He thinks he'll have a better idea in another month or so. Of course, you'll get an invitation. You're one of David's best friends."

David was Candice's older brother and currently on deployment with the Marines. Knowing that David and Barrett were friends put a pit in her stomach. She was beginning to realize that Barrett was very entangled with the Hunts. That was a complication she didn't need.

"I'd love to come to your wedding," Barrett said, giving her a pointed look. "Although, some people have suggested I'm not the best wedding guest these days."

She really needed to start thinking a bit more before she opened her mouth.

"Oh, I don't care about your cynical view of love," Candice proclaimed. "I know that Anthony and I have the real deal. We're going to be happy forever."

Barrett didn't refute her words, just stepped forward and gave her a hug. "I hope that's true. I'll let you all talk weddings." He nodded to Anthony. "Good luck."

Anthony smiled. "I've got Candice; that's all the luck I need."

"I shouldn't have brought up the wedding," Candice said, an odd look in her eyes, as her gaze followed Barrett's departure. "I hit a nerve."

"With Barrett?" she asked.

"He's a wonderful guy, but he had a hellish marriage, and things started to go bad as soon as he and his fiancée began planning the wedding. It was a beautiful event, but Barrett hates weddings now." She turned to Anthony. "That's not going to happen to us. We won't let the wedding get out of hand."

"I hope not," Anthony said. "But your mother is involved, so…"

She could hear the note of worry in Anthony's voice and wondered if Olivia would be trouble. Probably. She was definitely a woman who knew what she wanted and that was perfection.

"My mother may be involved, but it's our day."

Candice looked back at Kate. "You're going to have to keep my mom in check. I can never say no to her. She always wears me down. So, you will have to help me."

"Of course." She was beginning to wonder what she was getting herself into. "If you decide to hire me, I will do my best to make sure your day is exactly the way you want it."

"Which is why I want you," Candice said. "But we're going to have to play along with my mother's interview process, so she thinks I'm keeping an open mind. She's going to make demands, and you're going to have to meet a lot of them, because she's paying. She would much prefer to hire one of her friends, but I want this wedding to be mine, not hers."

"I understand."

"Good." Candice paused, tilting her head to the right. "How do you know Barrett? And did we interrupt something…down here on this quiet, dark patio?"

"No, not at all," she said hastily, not caring for the speculative gleam in Candice's eyes. "I was getting some air, and he had the same idea. I actually just met him earlier today."

"He's a great guy…in case you were wondering."

"Good to know, but I wasn't wondering," she said firmly.

"You'd be the first single woman to make that statement," Candice said with a short laugh. "Barrett is a hit with the ladies."

She decided to ignore that. "Let's talk about your wedding…"

--➤◄--

After a busy weekend getting her cupid statues moved into storage and catching up on paperwork, Kate headed into the office Monday afternoon after having spent the morning listening to wedding bands with one of her brides. The downstairs office door was closed, but she could hear hammering and voices. Apparently, Barrett had already started his remodel.

After he'd left her at the party, she hadn't seen him again, but she had to admit that he'd crossed her mind more than a few times. Hopefully, he'd appreciated finding his office empty of cupids when he arrived. That should move their bad start into at least neutral territory. Although, she wasn't thrilled with the dust or the noise. She had a bride coming by later in the day, and it wasn't exactly the ambiance she was going for. But she had no say about it. She certainly couldn't complain to the landlord.

The noise was a bit more muffled when she entered her office suite and closed the door, but it wasn't exactly quiet. "Has it been this bad all day?" she asked Shari.

"Pretty much. What are they doing downstairs?"

"I have no idea. But it sounds like they're moving walls. I can't imagine why. The office space was perfectly fine as it was."

"Apparently, not for a Fox," Shari said dryly. "Did you find any good bands?"

"No. And, for the record, the Devlin Sisters are not a pop group; they play heavy metal and would be better for a rave than a wedding reception. Do we have any aspirin?"

"Who would think a group called the Devlin Sisters would play heavy metal?" Shari asked in amazement, grabbing a bottle out of her desk and tossing it to her. "They sounded harmless."

"Believe me, they weren't. Although, they said they toned down for weddings. I can't imagine what their usual routine is. The little I saw included smashing a guitar over a drum set."

Shari laughed. "I thought you were going to start sending the brides out on their own to listen to bands."

"Thank goodness I didn't. Janine Hampton, Carol's mom, almost had heart failure when she saw the Devlin Sisters. If she'd been on her own, they might have had to call 911."

"Janine and her mother tend to overreact to most things."

"True. How was Tahoe?"

"Beautiful..." Shari winced at a sudden crash down below. "And more peaceful than here. How was the Hunts' party?"

"It was...interesting."

"Like fall in the pond or dump wine down your dress or run into a hot guy...interesting?"

She made a face at her. "When have any of those things happened?"

"Well, let's see, you fell into the wading pool at the Jacksons' engagement party."

"I was pushed by their six-year-old twins."

"And you dumped wine, not down your dress, but down Mrs. Bradington's white gown at her elegant soiree."

"Her drunken husband grabbed the bottle out of my hand, and he spilled the wine."

"And—"

"Stop already. The last thing I want to do is remember every embarrassing incident that has happened in the last few years. Besides, none of those things happened at the Hunts' party."

"Not even the hot guy?" Shari gave her a thoughtful look. "Or have I hit the nail on the head? You met someone, didn't you?"

Kate shook her head, not really wanting to get into her very brief conversation with Barrett Fox. "No. And there's nothing to tell. I spoke to Olivia and Candice, and I think they're genuinely interested in using us. They want to set up a meeting this week."

"Great."

"I'm going to start work on their proposal now."

"Before you do that…we have one more problem. Our downstairs neighbor wants our pink-and-white wedding wallpaper removed from the entry and stairwell."

"That's ridiculous. We got permission from his company to put up our wallpaper when we moved in."

"Some woman who calls herself his assistant says that it's inappropriate for his business," Shari replied. "She called a short while ago."

"Well, then he should just take his business back to wherever he had it before. I am not removing that wallpaper. This is just ridiculous. I already spent a fortune moving the cupids, and now we have to live through his remodel. It's too much."

"I don't think we have a choice. He's the landlord."

"We'll see about that," she said, knowing that with her splitting headache and her inexplicable desire to see Barrett again, she probably should not go downstairs. But she couldn't stop herself.

After several knocks on his door went unanswered, she pushed it open. There were two guys pulling down sheetrock, and she could see Barrett standing in the larger office by the front windows. He appeared to be putting together a bookshelf, which seemed a bit odd, but she was too irritated to think about that.

She moved quickly into the inner office. "We need to talk," she said. "Now."

He slowly turned his head, an odd look in his eyes. "Hello, Kate. How are you?"

"How am I?" she sputtered. "I'm extremely annoyed."

"Why?"

She frowned at his calm question. "Because you are turning everything upside down. I have clients coming to my office this afternoon and the stairwell is covered in dust, not to mention the fact that we can hardly hear ourselves think. And now I find out you want us to remove our very expensive wallpaper."

"Yes, that has to go. It's not appropriate for my business."

"How can wallpaper interfere with your business? And why are you renovating this office? If you don't like it, surely, you have another space you can use in some modern downtown building. Why wreck this beautiful, charming historic space?" she demanded, tapping her foot on the floor impatiently.

"This space suits me. It's private, and I think my clients will like that."

"Your clients? I don't understand. Doesn't Fox Management deal in real estate?"

"Among other things. But Fox Management is run by my father and brother. I'm an attorney—a divorce attorney. And I don't think your wedding wallpaper will make my clients happy."

She stared at him in astonishment. "You're

kidding."

"Why would I be kidding?"

"Because I can't imagine why on earth you would want to move your offices right downstairs from a wedding planning firm."

"I didn't know about your business when I made the decision to move. My current office was recently damaged by a water leak. This is the only place available that fits my needs. So, for the next several months, this will be my new home."

She shook her head. "This is not going to work. I don't want my brides exposed to the senseless bickering of divorce clients."

His lips twisted in an ironic smile. "I feel the same way, only in reverse. No one wants to be reminded of their wedding day when they're getting a divorce. I think the best thing we can do is to stay as separate as possible, and the common areas should be decorated in neutral colors."

"The wallpaper that's up is very subtle."

"Not subtle enough. We have to coexist. We have to compromise."

"I seem to be the one doing all the compromising," she said.

"Well, my family's company does own the building."

"So, you keep reminding me."

"It will be fine. In fact, we may both increase our business. You'll get them on the way in, and I'll get them on the way out."

She didn't find his cynical humor at all amusing. "That's not funny."

"It's true."

"Not everyone gets divorced."

"And not everyone lives happily ever after. In fact, most people don't. The statistics would agree with me."

"I'm not interested in statistics."

"Why would you be? You make your money on foolishly-in-love brides and grooms," he pointed out.

"It's not just about making money. I'm trying to make people happy, to kick off their marriage in the best way possible, to give them a day to remember."

"That day might be the only thing they want to remember."

"I'm not taking down the wallpaper."

"Then I'll have it done," he returned.

"You're extremely..." She couldn't find the appropriate word.

He gave her a mocking smile. "I was thinking the same thing about you."

"I was hoping we could be good neighbors, maybe even friends, but you're making that impossible."

"There are a lot of things we might be, but I don't think friends is one of them," he returned, giving her a look that sent an odd shiver down her spine.

She wished she had a snappy comeback, but she couldn't seem to find her voice. There was so much tension between them, and it wasn't all about their jobs or their opposing views. It was about an unexpected, unwelcome attraction. *She could not possibly desire someone she didn't even like, could she?*

"I should go," she said.

"You should," he agreed. "I have a lot to do."

"So do I."

"Then..."

Wondering why it was so difficult to walk away from him, she finally forced her feet to move, taking a little delight in slamming the door to his office behind her. But she didn't think a closed door was going to stop Barrett from continuing to turn her life upside down, and she wasn't just talking about wallpaper.

Chapter Three

Kate was one beautiful, stubborn, romantic spitfire, who was no doubt going to bring nothing but trouble into his life. Barrett smiled to himself, as he ran a hand through his hair and stared out the window. He should really keep her at arm's length, but when she'd been ranting on about happily ever after, his thoughts had gone more in the direction of pulling her into his arms and kissing her into quiet.

He could only imagine how that would have gone. She probably would have slapped his face. On the other hand, the way she'd looked at him with her beautiful blue eyes…well, he had a feeling she'd been feeling some of the same heat. Even though she clearly did not want to feel anything for him.

He stood against everything she believed in—and vice versa. The last person he needed in his life was some dreamy-eyed woman who wanted a fairy tale. He didn't deal in that kind of optimism anymore.

And Kate certainly didn't deal in his brand of

cynicism. She couldn't even handle ripping down some corny wallpaper. She'd acted like he wanted her to rip her heart out.

No. She was too much of everything.

He needed to stick with women who were on the same page as he was.

The door to his office opened. His heart gave a ridiculous leap at the idea that Kate might have come back for round two. But it was his younger brother, Matthew Fox, who walked over the threshold.

Matthew and he shared similar features, with brown hair and green eyes, but that's where their likeness ended. Matthew was an outgoing, talkative salesman, who liked nothing better than entertaining and closing a deal. He also enjoyed a lavish lifestyle, the result of those deals.

There was no question that Matt was his parents' favorite. Matt was the one who'd gone into the family business, who now worked with his dad, who played golf at the club and loved a good party. Whereas he didn't like golf, parties, or the business.

But he did like his brother.

"Matt. What are you doing down here?"

"Checking out your new digs. Not exactly a step up from your last place. Why didn't you stay at the tower? We've got plenty of room on the thirty-sixth floor."

"I like to keep my feet a little closer to the ground. A couple of days there was all I needed."

"Too close to Dad?"

"That was one of the reasons I decided to leave sooner rather than later."

Matthew grinned. "Understood. But this old Victorian should be housing a tea shop, not a law firm, not that you have much of a firm, since it's only you. And did I see that the upstairs office is a wedding planning company?"

"Yes, it is."

"How's that going to work with your business?"

"I have no idea. I didn't realize what the company was until I came by on Friday night." He shrugged. "It will work out. So, what are you doing here?"

"I'm here for Mom."

He groaned. "What party do I need to be at now?"

"The Winter Ball on Friday night. Mom wants you to take the daughter of her best friend Karen Cummings. Karen's daughter, Elaine, is in town and is dying to go to the party. She needs an escort—you."

"Why don't you take her?"

"I can't. I already have a date, but you do not."

He let out a groan. "I do not want to go to that party."

"I don't think you have a choice."

"Let me guess—Elaine is single."

"Definitely. But she's also very attractive, so this might not be bad, as setups go."

"Mom needs to concentrate on setting you up. I already went down the aisle once. It's your turn."

"No, thank you. I am enjoying my life as it is. Plus, I'm only thirty, whereas you are pushing thirty-four. Mom wants grandchildren."

"Well, I hope you're planning on procreating, because I'm not."

Matt frowned. "I hope that's not true. You'd make a great father."

"That would require being a husband, and I was not good at that—kind of like our old man." Their parents had divorced when they were young teenagers. His mom was on her second marriage, his father on his fourth.

"You're nothing like Dad. And Vanessa was not right for you. Next time, you'll make a better choice."

"There won't be a next time. I'm not interested in marriage. I certainly don't see a lot of happy ones in my line of work, or in my own life."

"I get it, but I still think the right woman might change your mind. At any rate, are you up for the Winter Ball? Before you say no, Mom told me to remind you that you owe her."

"Damn. I do owe her. She sent me a very lucrative client a few weeks back."

"Then it looks like you have a date Friday night. You might like her." Matt paused. "Unless there's someone else you're interested in…"

Kate's pretty blue eyes passed through his mind.

"Wait a second," Matt said, a gleam entering his gaze. "There is someone—who?"

"No one. Nobody," he said quickly.

"You're holding out on me. You've got someone on your mind."

"I'm not holding out on you. I barely know her." The words slipped out before he could stop them.

"*Her*? Does she have a name?"

"Not that you need to know. Look, I'll take Mom's friend's daughter to the party. But, right now, I need to get this bookcase put together, so unless you want to help…"

"God, no," Matt said with a laugh. "You know I'm not handy with tools."

"You could be."

"I don't want to be."

He smiled. That was another thing they had in

common—they both knew exactly what they wanted. And they usually knew how to get it.

But as his brother left the room, he reminded himself that not everything he wanted was good for him and getting involved with the tenant upstairs would be a really bad decision.

Although, it might be interesting...

———

"That man is the most obnoxious man I have ever met in my life," Kate declared, pacing back and forth in front of Shari's desk. She'd had a good twenty minutes to calm down, while Shari had been on the phone with a client, but she'd only gotten more annoyed with each passing minute.

"I guess he still wants the wallpaper removed."

"Do you know what he does for a living?" She didn't wait for an answer. "He is an attorney, but not just any kind of attorney. He is a bloodsucking, greedy, cynical divorce attorney."

"Really? I thought he worked for Fox Management."

"He said that's his family's company. Breaking up marriages is his real profession."

Shari frowned at her description. "I don't think you can blame a divorce on the attorney."

"Maybe not. But I've never met an attorney who tried to help the couple work out their problems. They're too busy looking for a way to make money."

Shari raised an eyebrow. "He is really annoying you."

"This is just crazy." She waved her hand in the air. "How can a divorce attorney and a wedding consultant share the same office building?"

"It is ironic, but you need to try to calm down. The Simpsons will be here in five minutes. And you have a full schedule the rest of the day."

"You're right. I'm just so mad. That man is…"

"Really getting under your skin," Shari finished.

"I want him gone."

"Are you sure that's what you want? Because I've never seen you this worked up over a guy."

"You haven't met Barrett Fox."

"No, but I'd really like to," Shari said with a gleam in her eyes.

"He's going to be bad for our business."

"We'll make it work. It's not like we have another choice. We have a lease. And this is a great location for us."

She really hated that Shari was making so much sense. "I know you're right. I just don't like it."

Shari gave her a thoughtful look. "What's really bothering you, Kate? You're always the cool, calm, poised person. You soothe anxious brides and work your magic on controlling moms. You can handle one cynical divorce attorney."

"I know I can. But he made fun of my business. He thinks I'm creating a wedding day that no marriage could ever live up to. He blames over-the-top weddings for the increasing divorce rate. They set expectations too high. The bride and groom aren't living in reality but in a dream world."

"But you don't believe that."

"No, I don't, but he did make a point." Not that she'd admitted that to him. In fact, she'd denied that any of her wedding clients had problems, but that wasn't completely true. "Look at Gretchen's wedding last year—it was completely over-the-top, and now she and Joel are talking about a separation. Was I part of the problem?"

"Gretchen is a looney tune. Forgive my bluntness, but it's true. Joel just took a long time to figure that out. You give people their dream, and that's a wonderful thing. You create happiness. You bring lovers together. Barrett Fox just cleans up after the ones that don't work."

"You're right. And you and Todd are still happy together, and you were my second client four years ago, so that's saying something. I don't know why he made me doubt myself."

"I don't, either, because you never doubt yourself. You've been single-minded and focused since I met you. It's been all business all the time."

She had a feeling that was part of the problem. With her last two friends getting married, she was beginning to wonder if she'd put too much time into her business and not enough into her personal life. She was starting to question a lot of her decisions. But regardless of whether or not she worked too much, she loved her job. And it was time to get back to doing it.

"I'm going to review the Simpson file. I'll be in the conference room."

"I'll send them in when they arrive. And, Kate, if you ever need to talk, I know I'm not one of your girlfriends from college, but I am here."

"You are one of my best friends as well as my right-hand person. I couldn't do this without you. I know I don't say that enough."

"We're good." The phone rang at the end of Shari's statement. "Back to work."

"Back to work," she echoed, happy with that

thought. She knew how to work. It was what she was good at it, and the rest of her life would just have to figure itself out.

Chapter Four

Barrett stopped by his office late Friday afternoon to check in on the remodel. To his relief, everything was done. The walls were painted, and the new carpet installed. Warm lighting bathed the rooms, and the furniture had been delivered and set up. His first client would be coming in on Monday, and he was ready for business.

However, as he considered the sleek couch and glass coffee table in the reception area, he found himself wondering if he might have gone a little too modern. This décor had probably fit better in the downtown office he'd previously inhabited, rather than this old Victorian with its nooks and curves, some of which he'd had recently eliminated.

Modern was good, he reminded himself with a frown, hating that Kate's voice had gotten into his head. And it wasn't just her voice, either; it was her fiery blue eyes, dark hair, and beautiful curves. Yeah, he'd definitely spent way too much time thinking about her the past week. He hadn't actually seen her since she'd stormed out of his office several days earlier, but he'd been acutely aware of footsteps overhead and the occasional melodic laughter that drifted down the stairway.

He tensed as he heard the outside door to the building open and then close, followed by a knock on his door. He walked over to open it, mentally preparing himself to go another round with Kate, who would no doubt have noticed the new wallpaper that had gone up in the entry and stairwell the night before. But it was an attractive redhead standing in the hall.

"Can I help you?" he asked.

"I'm Shari. I work upstairs with Kate. I thought I'd say hello. I assume you're Mr. Fox?"

"Barrett Fox," he said, shaking her hand.

"It's good to meet you."

"Is it?" he couldn't help asking.

Shari grinned. "I know you and Kate didn't get off on the right foot, but the cupid statues were more my fault than hers. I was the one who placed the order, and I was the one who suggested we store them down here." She glanced past him. "Wow, you've really changed everything, and in only a couple of days."

He moved back as she stepped inside. "It needed a facelift."

"It looks very…sophisticated…much like you. Although, I assume you don't always wear a tuxedo to work. I suspect I've caught you on your way somewhere."

"The Winter Ball. My date is meeting me here."

"That should be fun. I've heard it's an amazing party."

He shrugged. "We'll see."

"Well, I won't keep you." She turned to leave, then paused. "Will you be working here alone?"

"No. I have a paralegal assisting me—Jackie Carpenter. She'll be starting Monday."

"I look forward to meeting her." Shari paused. "I understand you're a divorce attorney."

"I am."

"Do you represent the women or the men?"

"It depends on the case, who wants to hire me, and how well I think we'd work together."

There was an odd look on Shari's face. "That makes sense."

"Do you know someone who might need a divorce attorney?" he asked.

"Maybe. I don't know yet. Do you take on new clients?"

"All the time."

"Are you good?" she asked bluntly.

"Very good," he returned.

She smiled. "I like your confidence."

"I think Kate called it arrogance."

"You did rub her the wrong way. She's been muttering under her breath all week."

Shari had no idea how much he wanted to rub Kate the right way. He cleared his throat at that errant thought. "I'm happy to offer your friend or you a complimentary consult."

"Why do you think it's me?"

"Something about the way you phrased the question. Am I wrong?"

Guilt flashed through her gaze. "My husband and I are having problems. But please don't share that with Kate. You rattled her the other day about creating too perfect weddings that make the subsequent marriage look boring and result in divorce."

"She planned your wedding?"

"I was her second client. And it was a great wedding. I had a tight budget, and she worked within it and still gave me the day of my dreams. My marital problems have nothing to do with the wedding day. Todd and I are just going in different directions. We went to Lake Tahoe over the weekend to try to work things out, but we didn't get very far. I think there might be another woman, but I don't know." She paused, shaking her head in bemusement. "I can't quite believe I just told you all that. We met thirty seconds ago. I haven't even told my parents or my friends."

"Sometimes it's easier to talk to someone you don't know."

"That's true. I feel like I'll be judged by everyone else. Maybe I'm not trying hard enough, or I should give it more time, or I'm imagining things. That's what Todd says. I don't know. I have a bad feeling."

"One thing I do know is that trusting yourself is the absolute best thing you can do."

"Kate said you're also divorced."

"My marriage lasted fifteen months, and, yes, I also had the feeling that maybe I should have tried harder or for longer, but it wouldn't have made a difference. I'm certain of that now. She's happier without me, and I am happier without her. Some relationships just don't last."

"Thanks for listening." She paused as the outer door opened. "That must be your date."

"Or Kate?" he suggested. He hadn't seen her since Monday, but she'd been on his mind a lot.

"I hope it's not Kate. She'll think I'm consorting with the enemy."

"I don't think our conversation qualifies as consorting. And I really don't want to be the enemy."

"Then stop making Kate take down anything that smacks of romance. If you go after the picture of the two swans by the front door, it will be war."

"I'll keep that in mind," he said, seeing not Kate, but one of his clients, Monica Harding, come through the door.

"I'll let you go," Shari said.

"Thanks for stopping in."

"Sure," Shari said, as she moved out of the office.

"I know I don't have an appointment, Barrett, and I'm not supposed to see you until Monday, but I have to talk to you," Monica said, dabbing at her red eyes with a tissue. "Do you have some time?"

"About fifteen minutes," he said, checking his watch. "I'm meeting someone."

"That's why you're wearing a tux. It reminds me of my wedding. John looked so handsome in his tux. I didn't know it was going to end." She burst into sobs.

His heart sank. While drama wasn't an unusual part of his job, he'd never been good with tears, and he was already regretting taking Monica on as a client. Her emotions were almost manic in their extremes. One minute she was sad, the next she was angry, and sometimes she even went on a frantic, happy rant about how her life would be so much better once she got her cheating husband out of her life.

"Let's go into my office," he suggested.

"How can I hate someone I used to love?" she asked, between gulps for breath.

He didn't reply. He'd learned a long time ago that

that was not a question that had a good answer.

———»»««———

"You were right about the man downstairs," Shari said, as she entered Kate's office.

Kate raised her gaze from the catering bid she'd been studying. "That he's obnoxious, arrogant and rude?"

"That he's gorgeous—tall, handsome, and sexy...especially in a tuxedo."

"He was wearing a tuxedo?"

"He's going to the Winter Ball. I've always wanted to go to that."

She wasn't surprised that Barrett had made the guest list. He was definitely in that league. "Barrett might look nice on the outside, but he is not nice on the inside."

"He was actually pretty friendly."

"You talked to him?" She felt a little betrayed.

"I wanted to introduce myself. And don't look at me like I just crossed into enemy territory. We don't want to be at war with our landlord."

She frowned, knowing Shari made a good point. "What did he tell you to rip down now? If he goes after my swan photo, I swear—"

"I already told him that's your red line." Shari perched on the arm of the chair in front of her desk. "His office is very modern and sophisticated. I can't believe the renovations were done so quickly."

"Apparently, money makes things move faster. I'm sure it's nice, but it doesn't sound like it fits this historic old house."

"Not exactly," Shari admitted. "But it's personal

taste. Anyway, I'm going to run some checks down to the bank, and then I'll head home. You just have Jennifer, right?"

"Yes. She wants to bring her wedding dress by to show me how impossible it's going to be for her to wear it."

"Why? What's wrong with it?"

"It belonged to her deceased mother, who was a Southern belle, and the dress is meant to be worn over a hoop skirt."

"But Jennifer is twenty-one and not really the hoop-skirt type."

"Yes, but her father wants Jennifer to wear it, saying it would mean so much to her mother, and Jennifer is very conflicted. I suggested she just wear it for the ceremony and then change into a contemporary gown for the reception."

"That seems reasonable."

"I hope she goes for it. I think she'll feel bad if she doesn't wear it."

Shari stood up as the bell attached to their office door rang. "That must be her. Good luck."

"Thanks." She set aside the information she'd been studying on next week's wedding, so she could take on Jennifer's problem, which appeared to be much bigger than she'd anticipated.

Jennifer, a willowy brunette, who always looked like she needed to eat, was practically crying as she entered the office with a big garment bag over her arm. "It's awful," Jennifer said. "I can't even walk in it, and I have to go down a long flight of stairs."

"What if your father walks you down the stairs, instead of meeting you at the bottom?" she suggested, as she got to her feet. The only thing besides the dress that Mr. Phillips had insisted on was that his daughter be married in his home, which unfortunately boasted a long and winding staircase.

"He said he wants me to have a moment. He thinks it will be beautiful and dramatic. It's the way my mother did it. I want to make him happy. I want to honor my mom, but I don't want to fall on my face in this not very pretty dress." Jennifer gave her a look filled with pain and guilt. She wanted to honor her mother, but she also wanted her own day. It was a difficult situation.

"It can't be that bad. Let's take a look." She unzipped the bag and pulled out the dress and the petticoat hoop. "The dress looks pretty," she said, trying not to look aghast at the enormous amount of fabric that would completely swamp Jennifer's thin frame.

"I could maybe wear the dress, but the hoop—no way. I tried putting it on and walking, and I took one step and tripped."

"Maybe you just need to practice a bit." She pulled the lacy hoop skirt on over her jeans and was surprised by the volume. She could see why it had put Jennifer off. It was one thing to look at it from afar than to look down at it. She couldn't even see her feet.

"It's awful," Jennifer said.

"Maybe not. Let's try this on the stairs." She glanced at the clock on her wall. It was after five and Shari had said that Barrett was on his way out.

"If you want to. But don't blame me if you break your neck."

"Hey, thousands of women have walked down stairs in hoop skirts. It can be done," she said optimistically, as they headed out of the office. As she looked down the narrow, steep staircase, she had to admit she was a little intimidated. But she needed to give Jennifer some confidence. Once she saw that it could be done, she wouldn't be so worried. "Why don't you wait at the bottom, so you can see my dramatic descent?"

"All right." Jennifer jogged down the stairs and waited by the front door. "Go ahead."

She drew in a deep breath and took the first step. After a couple of stairs, she began to breathe more easily. "It's not that bad."

"You do look sort of majestic. But you only have the hoop skirt on—not the dress, which makes everything bigger."

"I still think we can make it work." She was almost at the bottom of the stairs when Barrett's door flew open. She took one look at his incredulous face and tumbled down the last three steps, landing in an undignified heap at his feet.

Jennifer gasped in horror. "Oh, my God, are you all right, Kate?"

She tried to get up, but her legs were tangled in the hoop, and she couldn't even see over it.

A man's hand came into view. She really didn't want to take it, but Jennifer seemed to be paralyzed.

She put her hand into Barrett's, allowing him to help her to her feet. As if his mocking face wasn't enough embarrassment, behind him stood a beautiful blonde, who was close to six feet tall, wearing a tight white dress, and an expression of pure distaste.

"Are you hurt?" Barrett asked.

"Only my pride," she muttered. "You startled me. I would have been fine, otherwise." She looked at Jennifer. "Really, I would have been fine."

"If you call this fine," Barrett put in, "then you might need to redefine that word. What are you wearing?"

"It's a hoop skirt. It goes under a bridal gown. I was showing Jennifer that she would be able to walk down the stairs while wearing it."

A smile spread across his face. "You really do go above and beyond, don't you?"

"Barrett, can we go?" the woman asked impatiently.

"One second," he said, his gaze narrowing as he saw her rubbing her fingers. "Did you hurt your hand?"

"It's fine," she said, even though she could feel pain shooting through her fingers.

He frowned. "You should see a doctor."

"I just need some ice. Please go on with your evening."

"Barrett," the blonde said again, tapping her foot with impatience.

"I'm coming." He glanced at her. "Maybe take that skirt off before you go back up the stairs." He moved toward the door with his date, then paused, looking at Jennifer. "If you don't want to walk down the stairs in that thing, don't do it. It's your wedding. Always remember that."

She didn't particularly care for Barrett giving her client wedding advice, but she didn't really disagree with him.

As the door closed behind Barrett and his date, she turned to Jennifer. "I'm sorry I messed that up. He surprised me."

"I can't do it, Kate. I can't wear it. Maybe I should just call off the wedding. I don't want to hurt my father, but I can't be my mom for him. I can't relive his wedding day."

"You have to talk to him, Jennifer."

"He'll hate me."

"No. He loves you. I like tradition, and I like that you want to honor your mom. It's very sweet. But this is your day. If you want me to speak to your dad, I will, but I think it would be better if it came from you."

Jennifer drew in a breath. "You're right. I'll do it tonight. I'll tell him how I feel." She paused. "And, if you don't mind, I'm going to tell him about how you fell down the stairs, just to make my point a little stronger."

"Happy to be the sacrificial lamb," she said dryly, as she got out of the skirt.

After Jennifer had gathered her things together and left, Kate took a longer look at her hand. Her two middle fingers were swollen, and her entire wrist was aching. She really hoped she hadn't broken something. She and Liz were supposed to spend the evening putting together sample favors to show Maggie and Jessica tomorrow. Hopefully, some ice would help.

She grabbed her tote bag, threw in some work to take home, and then headed down the stairs. As she passed Barrett's office door, she was reminded of not only him but also the beautiful blonde at his side. Was she a girlfriend? Probably. She seemed to be exactly the kind of woman Barrett Fox would date: sophisticated, stylish, and a little snobby.

The woman certainly hadn't expressed any concern after she'd tumbled down the stairs. Instead, she'd been impatient and clearly irritated that Barrett was taking any time at all with a crazy woman in a hoop skirt.

She could only imagine the picture she'd made. At least she'd had on pants underneath the hoop. Her fall could have been even more humiliating.

She definitely didn't seem able to put her best foot forward when it came to Barrett. And she'd just given him something else to mock about her wedding business. Not that she made a habit of trying on her bride's dresses and parading down the stairs. On the other hand, she was willing to do whatever it took to make her clients happy, and Jennifer had needed to see her go down the stairs. Maybe the end result hadn't been what she'd planned on, but the incident had made Jennifer realize she needed to confront her father's expectations.

That was a positive step, and one that might not have happened without her help.

Taking solace in that thought, she locked the front door and walked down the street. Her apartment was about a mile away and up a few rather steep streets, which tonight seemed even more wearying than normal. Her hand was aching and worries about what she might not be able to get done with a real injury were stressing her out.

When she finally arrived at her small one-bedroom apartment, she immediately headed for the kitchen. She poured ice into a pitcher and then sat down on the couch and put her hand in the ice.

Pain shot all the way up her arm. She winced but hoped that the throbbing would go away as soon as the swelling went down.

Her phone buzzed, and she reached for her bag with her good hand and pulled it out. It was Liz, one of her college friends. "Hi, Liz, are you here already?"

"No, I'm actually at the hospital."

"What?" she asked in alarm. "Are you all right?"

"I'm fine but Michael broke his ankle."

"What happened?"

"He was riding his bike after work, and he hit a bump or something, and he went flying. He said it was a total klutz move, and he's furious with himself. Luckily, he had his helmet on, but he broke a bone in his foot, and he's getting a cast, so I'm not coming tonight."

"Of course not. I'm so sorry."

"He'll be fine. But I might have my hands full for a few days with the two males in my life. Josh is getting a tooth, so I'm pretty sure he and Michael will be cranky together."

She smiled to herself. "Do you want some help? Although, I might not be able to hold the baby right now—I hurt my hand at work. Michael is apparently not the only klutz."

"How bad is it?"

"Not sure yet. It's encased in ice at the moment. But I can still babysit if you need me."

"Michael's sister is watching Josh, so he's fine. At least we still have some time to get the favors done."

"Don't worry. It will all get done."

"You are the miracle maker, so I have no choice but to believe you," Liz said. "But I hope your hand isn't going to need a cast. Because you're not just planning Maggie and Jessica's wedding, you're going to be in it."

"I don't think anything is broken," she said, really hoping that was true. "I'll talk to you later. Take care of Michael."

"I will."

She set down her phone and pulled out her hand. Her fingers were still puffy, but the pain had diminished a little. She stuck her hand back in the ice and rested her head on the back of the couch, thinking this night wasn't going at all as she'd planned.

She wondered if Barrett was having a better time in his fancy tux with his fancy girlfriend...

Chapter Five

—➤➤❰❰◄—

The ballroom of the Worthington Hotel at the top of Nob Hill was packed with people, many of which Barrett knew, many of which he didn't really care to know. He took a long draught of beer, having passed on the endless flow of champagne, and watched his date flirt with one of the lawyers for Fox Management. Elaine was beautiful and had a killer body, but she was not at all interesting—at least not to him. Their conversation in the car had basically been a monologue about the number of social media followers she had accumulated. She'd even taken a few selfies in the car, which had made him nuts. He'd never understood the allure of constantly photographing yourself. And while Elaine's smile was sexy, it was also cold.

She hadn't cared one bit when Kate had come tumbling down the stairs. She'd practically stepped over her on the way to the door, and while Kate and he were hardly friends, he hoped she was all right.

The way she'd been holding her hand had belied her words that everything was fine.

"Here you are," his brother said, joining him with a curvy redhead by his side. "This is Amy—my brother, Barrett."

"Hi, Barrett," Amy said with a warm smile. "I hear your mother set you up."

"I see Matt's big mouth is still working."

His brother gave him an unrepentant grin. "How are things going?"

He tipped his head to where Elaine was now holding court in a circle of interested men. She was definitely a woman who liked to be the center of attention.

"I know her," Amy said. "That's Elaine Cummings. She's a fashion blogger and a social media influencer. She has hundreds of thousands of followers."

"She said a lot about that in the car," he admitted. "She's definitely doing some networking tonight."

"Would you guys excuse me? I'm going to use the ladies' room," Amy said. "I'll be back." She handed Matt her glass of champagne and then left them alone.

"Any sparks between you and Elaine?" Matt asked with a grin.

"Not a one. And I'm sure she feels the same way. She just wanted me to get her through the door, which I did. What about Amy? What's her story?"

"She's an interior designer. She's helping me furnish my new apartment."

He saw a gleam in his brother's eyes that he hadn't seen in a while. "You like her."

"I do," Matt admitted. "But it's early days. We've only gone out a few times. We'll see how it goes."

"Well, good for you."

"Sorry your date turned out to be a dud."

He shrugged. "I didn't have high expectations."

"Maybe that's the problem," Matt said cryptically.

"Whatever that means."

"It means it's time to get back in the game."

"I'm in the game."

"Are you?"

He frowned at his brother's challenging words. "I go out. I just haven't met anyone I want to see twice." As he finished speaking, his mind returned to Kate. He did want to see her again. But he told himself that was because he was concerned about her hand. With the way she felt about him, she might want to sue him for her fall. Not that she seemed like the litigious type. On the other hand, it would probably make sense to ensure she had the proper medical care.

"Barrett, are you listening to me?"

He actually had no idea what his brother had just said. "Sorry. What?"

"Your date is now slow dancing with David Bennis."

His gaze moved to the dance floor where Elaine and David were getting very close. Besides being a successful lawyer, David had deep pockets and blue blood running through his veins. Elaine certainly moved fast when she saw something or someone she wanted. He kind of admired that. "Good," he said. "I'm glad she's found someone to entertain her. I think I'll get going."

"Seriously?" Matt asked, raising his brow. "Where do you have to be?"

"I'm bored. I'm tired. I want to get out of here. Would you mind telling Elaine that I had to leave?

Make sure she has a ride to wherever she wants to go."

"I suppose I could do that, but you'll owe me."

"I'll happily pay, as long as it's not another blind date."

"So, you're just going home?" Matt asked, a speculative glint in his eyes.

"Where else would I be going?" he said lightly, as he headed to the door.

—————

Kate took her hand out of the second bucket of ice. She'd given herself a ten-minute break between icings while she'd changed into leggings and a long sweater and popped a frozen pizza into the oven.

Her fingers were red and slightly less puffy, but they were still painful. She looked at the pile of ribbons, lace, potpourri and other items on the kitchen table in front of her. She'd talked herself into the idea that she could at least get something done, if she just went slowly, but it was looking like a very formidable task. She'd wanted to show the samples to Jessica and Maggie tomorrow, but that might have to wait. She was just about to plunge her hand back into the ice, when her doorbell buzzer went off.

She wrapped a dishtowel around her wet hand and moved toward the intercom. "Hello?"

"It's Barrett. Can I come in?"

Her heart skipped a beat. "Uh, I guess. I'm on the second floor." She buzzed him in, then moved to open her door. She couldn't imagine why Barrett had come to see her. He was supposed to be at the Winter Ball.

Barrett came down the hall a moment later, still

wearing his tuxedo, which only reminded her that her casual wear was a little on the ragged side. "What do you want?" she snapped, annoyed that he'd caught her at her worst once again.

"I came to see if you were all right," he said, glancing at her towel-wrapped hand. "And you're not."

"It's not that bad."

"Let me see."

She unwrapped the towel and revealed her puffy fingers.

"You might have broken one or both of those fingers."

"They're not crooked just swollen. I'm hoping for the best."

"Instead of hoping, you should have someone take a look at it."

"I'm soaking it in ice. Everything will be fine in the morning."

"Why don't you want to see a doctor?" he asked curiously.

"Because I don't need to. Why are you here?"

"I wanted to check on you—see if you were all right."

She gave him a disbelieving look. "You were concerned about me?" Her gaze narrowed. "Oh, I get it. You think I'm going to sue you, don't you?"

"Never crossed my mind. If you're going to sue anyone, it would have to be the owner of that hoop thing you were wearing." He paused. "Can I come in?"

"Why?" As the word left her mouth, her oven timer went off.

"Whatever you're cooking smells good," Barrett

commented.

"It's just a frozen pizza."

"Big enough for two?"

"You want to share a frozen pizza with me while you're wearing a tuxedo? Why aren't you at the ball? Shari told me you were going. It can't be over. It's barely eight."

"It's not over, but I was done."

"What happened to your date?"

"You might want to get your pizza before it burns."

"Fine, come in," she said, leaving him to enter, as she moved into the kitchen and took out her pizza, setting it on the stovetop to cool.

Barrett followed her into the small kitchen. "Ah, it is big enough to share," he said with a smile that warmed his features and made her heart beat a little faster.

She couldn't argue with that. "Fine. We can share." She pulled out her pizza cutter. "You can slice. I'll get the plates."

"Don't hurt your hand."

"Thankfully, it's my left hand."

She put the plates on the counter and opened the refrigerator. "I have orange juice, milk, and sparkling water."

"I'll take the water," he said, as he placed a couple of slices of pizza on each plate, then took them over to the table, which was laden with wedding supplies. "What is all this?"

"I'm supposed to be making wedding favors tonight. You can just push them to one side."

"You really take your work home with you, don't you?"

"There's always a lot to do."

She set a large bottle of water on the table. "If you don't mind opening this, I'll get some glasses."

After putting the glasses down, she took a seat across from him. "I hope you don't get tomato sauce on that tuxedo."

"I think I can manage, but it can always be cleaned."

"So, you own it."

"I prefer to own over renting."

"Nice if you can afford it," she commented, taking a bite of her pizza.

"This is good," Barrett said, devouring his first piece in a few bites.

"You really were hungry. Don't they feed you at the Winter Ball?"

"There were trays going by, but I'm not a fan of weird finger food and people kept wanting to talk to me," he complained.

"Poor you. Too much fancy food and too many people who like you. Although, why you're popular is a mystery to me," she said dryly.

He smiled. "We haven't gotten off to a good start."

"Which is your fault," she pointed out.

"Maybe we can reset. Since we're going to be work neighbors, it would be easier if we got along."

"I suppose. What happened to your beautiful date?"

"She's still at the party, networking to her heart's delight."

"Networking? That doesn't sound very romantic."

"Tonight's date wasn't about romance. Elaine is one of my mother's setups. She wants me to get married again, and she keeps throwing eligible women my way. However, Elaine was not at all interested in me, especially when she realized I have no intention of ever getting married again."

"Did you tell her that? Because that's quite a statement for a first date. And usually not one you make if you want a second date."

"I didn't want a second date. I didn't want the first date. And I think I slid it in somewhere in the middle of her monologue about her social media influence."

"Oh, she's one of those."

"Elaine loves the selfie."

She nodded in complete understanding. "Well, I can't say I'm sorry she won't be showing up at your office. She didn't seem like a very caring person when I tumbled down the stairs and landed at your feet. She stepped over me like I was roadkill."

"In a lot of lace," he said with a grin. "Elaine is an ambitious social climber. Trust me, she's having a better time at the party without me."

"Was the ball amazing? I've heard it's fabulous."

He shrugged. "It was all right."

"Speaks the man who has probably been a dozen times."

"Probably." He finished his slice of pizza and tipped his head toward the pile of supplies hovering by his elbow. "Why don't you farm out the wedding favor construction? Surely, you can find an intern or an assistant to do it."

"I don't normally make the favors. We have a group of high school girls who usually work on them, but these are for the double wedding of two of my best friends, Jessica and Maggie. I'm not just planning their wedding; I'm also in it. And it needs to be perfect. I told my friends I'd show them the samples tomorrow when we meet for lunch. Another bridesmaid, Liz, was supposed to come by tonight to help me, but her husband fell off his bike and she ended up at the ER with him. Thankfully, he's all right, but she needs to take care of him." She blew out a breath. "And that was probably way more than you wanted to know."

"With your hand, I don't think you're going to get too far on your own."

"I just need to get six samples done. I can soldier through."

He gave her a doubtful look. "You really think you can manage?"

"I'll figure it out." She paused, taking a sip of her water. "How did you know where I live?"

"I have your home address on the lease you signed with us."

"Oh, right. So, there really wasn't any other office space in the vast Fox Management empire that you could have used?"

"The Union Street location is convenient for me. I live in the Marina. I can walk to work."

"But surely your well-to-do clients would prefer a more sophisticated office building."

He shrugged. "I know you'd like to be rid of me, but that won't happen for at least six months. You're going to have to soldier on there, too."

"Just don't take down the swan picture by the front door."

"What is the deal with that picture?"

"My grandparents gave it to me. It's their love story."

"They're swans?" he asked, with a sparkle in his

green eyes.

"Ha-ha. No, but they are mated for life, like the swans. They've been together for fifty-five years, and they love each other as much now as they did the day they married."

"That's something."

"True love does exist, and weddings don't always kill a marriage," she said pointedly.

"What kind of wedding did they have?"

"They got married in a small church in Portola Valley. My grandmother had grown up in the area and had always wanted to get married there. The reception was in the church hall. There was a cake, flowers, music. There might have only been about twenty-five guests, but my grandmother says it was perfect."

"Well, good for them."

"What about your parents, grandparents? Are they together?" she asked curiously.

"I only have one grandmother left, and she's been married three times. My mother has been married twice, and my father is on his fourth marriage. His brides keep getting younger and younger."

"Wow, that's a lot of marriages."

"And weddings. Each and every one of them has spent a great deal of money to have the perfect day, only to end up with an imperfect marriage."

"Again, you're generalizing."

"Not when it comes to my family. Apparently, the Foxes are not cut out for marriage."

"Maybe it's more about picking the right person than the right wedding venue."

"I'll give you that. What about your parents? What's their story? Have they been as happily married as your grandparents?"

She frowned at his question, not really wanting to answer it, because it would just add fuel to his fire when it came to weddings and marriage. "Do you want more pizza? There are a few slices left."

"You don't want to tell me about your parents. Why?"

She didn't like the knowing gleam in his eyes. "I just thought you might still be hungry. I was being a good host."

"They're divorced, aren't they?"

"No, they're not divorced."

"Really?" Surprise ran across his face. "Then why did you hesitate to answer the question?"

She really didn't need to tell him her life story. But for some reason it was difficult to look away from him. "My parents aren't divorced, because they were never married. My mom got pregnant. My dad hung around until I was born and then he took off. He said he couldn't be a father. He didn't want me in his life."

Barrett's humor faded. "I'm sorry, Kate."

She shrugged. "It's not that big of a deal. I never knew him. How can you miss something you never had?"

"Some men aren't cut out to be fathers. I'm sure it wasn't personal to you."

"When your father rejects you, it feels personal."

"He didn't know you."

"He didn't want to know me. Anyway, that's their story."

"Are you close with your mother?"

"No. She also wasn't cut out to be a parent. She's a singer, and she has been in and out of my life— mostly out. I lived with my grandparents from the time I was six until I went to college. They raised me.

They're the people I count on."

"Do they live here in the city?"

"No. They're in Berkeley. They have a small house in the hills. It's not much, but it has a great view of the city. I used to sit on the patio and think about one day living in San Francisco and having my own business."

"It all came true."

"Yes. Dreams can come true. And marriages can last. My parents didn't even try, but my grandparents are great role models."

He smiled. "You're clearly an optimist."

"And you are clearly not."

"Sometimes optimism is unwarranted. You need to be realistic, and I'm not talking about love and romance right now."

"What are you talking about?" she asked warily.

"Your fingers. I think at least one of them is broken. You can't wish that away with happy thoughts."

As she turned her gaze on her hand, she was afraid he might be right.

"Let me take you to the ER," Barrett said.

"If the swelling doesn't subside, I'll go in the morning. There's not much they can do anyway. Do you want more pizza?"

"I'm full. It was very good."

"I can't take much credit. All I did was put it in the oven. I'm afraid I don't do much cooking."

"When would you have time? Dealing with brides, trying on wedding skirts, making favors…"

"It is busy, but I love it. And I'm lucky I get to do what I love."

He nodded, giving her a thoughtful look. "You

are lucky. Did you always want to be a wedding planner?"

"Yes. It was an idea I had really young. When I was in college, I worked for a caterer, and after college, I moonlighted at a florist shop, while I worked as an account manager at an advertising agency for my very boring day job. But my ultimate goal was to be a wedding planner. Luckily, I made some contacts at the florist, who did a lot of weddings, and eventually I was able to quit the ad agency and start up my own little company. The first two years were rough, but business is starting to boom now. Getting Candice Hunt's wedding would be my biggest job yet. Although, I'm not sure she'll end up hiring me."

"Why wouldn't she?"

"Her mother would prefer to hire one of her friends, and in the end, whoever pays the checks usually has the most say. But I'm meeting with both of them next Friday, so we'll see if they like my proposal."

"You have a lot on your plate."

"I like it that way."

"So do I," he admitted. "Work is where I'm at my best."

"Unlike the Winter Ball, where you left your very attractive date without an escort."

He tipped his head. "She had already moved on to someone else before I left. And big, expensive parties are not really my thing."

"And yet you've been to two in the last week—if you count the Hunts' party."

"The Hunts have been longtime friends. The Winter Ball was not my idea, but sometimes I try to keep my mother happy."

"Only sometimes?"

"She's not an easy woman to please. It takes a lot of effort, and the results are usually not good—at least not for me. My brother is much better at charming her into a better mood."

"Younger or older brother?"

"Younger. Matt is great. He's the perfect son, too. He's going to take over Fox Management one day. My parents are very proud."

"I'm sure they're proud of you, too."

"I'm not sure pride is the first word that comes to mind when they think of me. I let them down with my divorce and my career choices," he replied.

"You have to live your life, not theirs."

"Now that I agree with. See, we're getting along better already."

"I have to admit you're nicer than I thought."

He smiled. "So nice, I'm going to help you."

"Help me do what?"

"Make your sample favors."

She stared at him in surprise. "Are you serious? You want to fill little satin bags with potpourri?"

"Is that what the favor is?"

"It's one of them."

"You know that the guys at the wedding don't give a crap about potpourri."

"Well, the ladies do."

"And the bride calls the shots," he said, an edge of bitterness in his tone.

"What were your favors?"

"Some kind of perfumed package. I didn't pay much attention."

She got up and reached across the table with her

good hand to grab a bag of items she'd picked up at the party store. "I know you don't like potpourri; what do you think about dice, cards, and shot glasses?"

"I'm getting a little more interested," he said, as she set the items in front of him.

"Maggie and Jessica are doing both male and female favors. Like you, their grooms weren't interested in potpourri."

"What else have you got?"

"Tiny personalized bottles of Jack Daniel's." She pushed one across to him and saw the gleam of approval in his eyes.

"Nice."

"I also have a key chain bar tool and samples of men's cologne. I just need to put them in some small boxes and tie them with ribbon and put on a seal, that kind of thing."

"What are you doing for the ladies?"

"I have rustic heart favor boxes that hold a small heart-shaped candle, perfume samples, a gold heart bottle stopper, individually wrapped chocolate truffles, and some potpourri."

"Let's do it. Let's put them together. Just tell me what to do."

"You're really going to do this?"

"Consider it a gesture of good will."

"All right. I won't say no." She pushed the small boxes that needed to be put together across the table, while she started cutting ribbon to tie the satin bags holding one of the female-oriented favors.

Barrett put all his attention on the project at hand, while she was more than a little distracted by his presence, caught up in the warm, spicy scent of his aftershave, the way his dark hair fell over his forehead. He was certainly a handsome man, but also a man of contradictions: cool and sophisticated, but also friendly and down-to-earth. She didn't quite know what to make of him.

Barrett had been working for nearly thirty minutes when the potpourri favor he was putting together suddenly fell apart in his hands, the lace and ribbons falling to the floor.

Instinctively they both reached for the favor at the same time, but as Kate grasped the lace, Barrett caught her arm. His warm touch sent her emotions spinning. She looked into his eyes, and her heart seemed to stop. Slowly they straightened, their eyes locked in a gaze of unmistakable attraction.

Barrett pulled her good hand to his lips, never taking his eyes off her face. He kissed her palm, and his tongue moved gently over her fingers, leaving her hot with desire. She felt herself drifting toward him, closer and closer until their faces were inches apart. She could see the faint shadow of his beard, the tiny laugh lines around his eyes. She noted every detail in that split second before his lips touched hers.

A wave of heat rushed through her and she found herself kissing him back as his hand slid around her neck and he pulled her closer.

And then the loud squealing of her cuckoo clock made them both jump back, effectively dousing the fire between them.

"What the hell was that?" Barrett demanded.

"My clock," she said faintly, straightening up in her chair. She tipped her head toward the cuckoo clock on the kitchen wall.

He looked at it in bemusement, then turned back to her. "You have a cuckoo clock? I didn't think those existed anymore."

"It was my grandparents' clock. They gave it to me as a housewarming present."

"It's loud."

"It has charm," she defended. "And it keeps very good time."

"Maybe so, but it has a lousy sense of timing," he remarked regretfully.

She stared back at him, filled with mixed emotions. She wanted to keep going on with that kiss, but her brain was screaming caution. "Or maybe a good sense of timing," she murmured. "We have to work in the same building, and I'm not sure this truce could take another kiss like that. It would complicate things."

"It would do that," he agreed, but the glitter in his eyes told her how much he wanted to keep going.

She cleared her throat. "I can finish the last favor on my own." She stood up. "You've done more than enough."

"I guess that's my cue to leave," he said, as he rose.

"Thanks, Barrett. You were a lifesaver."

"You're welcome." He gave her a long look. "You're not anything like I first thought."

"I could say the same about you," she replied.

He nodded. "Well, I guess I'll see you around the building."

"I'll try not to fall at your feet again."

A smile curved his lips. "I have a feeling that our next meeting will be just as memorable."

"Why would you say that?"

"Judging by our past history, I'd say the excitement is just beginning."

She decided not to touch that comment, because she had a feeling he was right.

She walked him to the door and tried not to think about giving in to a crazy attraction burning between them. She pushed him into the hall and locked the door behind him, then leaned against the solid frame and let out a breath. She hadn't felt so worked up by a man in a very long time.

But it could not be this man. He was her landlord, her office neighbor, but more than that, he was cynical and cocky and not at all the kind of man she wanted in her life.

She just wished he wasn't so damn attractive.

Chapter Six

—→→➤◄◄◄—

"And then I toppled down the stairs, jamming and spraining my fingers in the process." Kate extended her hand for Maggie and Jessica to inspect. Her middle two fingers were in a splint. She'd stopped by the ER just past eight to get an X-ray, but luckily nothing was broken.

After that, she'd crammed in visits to a wedding caterer and a photographer before meeting up with Jessica and Maggie for a late lunch on Chestnut Street in the Marina.

"That looks painful," Maggie said.

"It's better today."

"I can't believe you had to show a bride how to walk down a staircase in a hoop skirt," Jessica said with a laugh. "There is no limit to what you will do to make someone happy. You really go above and beyond, Kate."

"It wasn't my best idea." She paused as the waitress set down three glasses of iced tea. "But despite my hand, I did manage to get your favors done."

"How on earth did you do that?" Maggie asked, her bright-blue eyes curious.

"Well, I had a little help."

"From Shari?"

"No." She suddenly realized that her funny story was going to lead to a lot of questions.

"Then who?" Jessica asked.

"Just a friend. I mean, not really a friend, but someone who helped."

"Okay, that sounds like a story," Jessica said, a curious gleam in her eyes. "Why are you being so vague?"

"Because the two of you are going to jump to conclusions."

"Like sexy conclusions?" Maggie asked.

"Was it a man?" Jessica added.

"It was a man. But it wasn't sexy. Well, it was kind of sexy. But nothing happened. Well, something almost happened, but it didn't."

Maggie laughed. "Kate, I haven't seen you this befuddled since you kissed Dax Holmes in our junior year of college."

Her face reddened at that memory. "Don't remind me. I thought Dax was trying to kiss me, but he was just leaning over to help me with my seat belt, which was stuck in the door. I thought he was making a move. It was so embarrassing. He had only asked me out because he wanted me to tutor him in math. He had the hots for that cheerleader, Dee Powell."

"You were way too good for Dax," Maggie said.

"Did you embarrass yourself last night, too?" Jessica asked. "Come on, spill."

She sighed, realizing she'd gone too far to backtrack. "Fine. When I fell down the stairs, I landed at the feet of my new landlord and fellow tenant, Barrett Fox. He was wearing a tuxedo and he was with a beautiful blonde. They were on their way to the Winter Ball. They looked glamorous, and I looked like an idiot."

"Wait, Barrett Fox as in Fox Management?" Maggie asked. "His father stayed at the Stratton a few years ago, but he was with a young wife. I doubt that was Barrett's mother."

"Barrett said his father has been married a couple of times."

"Well, that family is loaded. They took our best suite."

"Barrett is part of the family but not in the family business. He's a lawyer, and not just any lawyer—a divorce attorney. We've been battling it out since he moved in, because his clients and my clients are on the opposite ends of bridal bliss," she said.

"Get back to what happened last night," Maggie urged.

"Barrett was concerned about me after my fall, so he stopped by my apartment after he left the ball."

"What happened to the beautiful blonde?" Maggie asked.

"He said she was just a setup. They didn't know each other. I'm sure he came by to make certain I wasn't thinking of suing him."

"And…" Jessica prodded.

"And he wound up staying to share my frozen pizza. He was hungry, and it was ready. He actually turned out to be nicer than I thought. He helped me put the favors together, since my hand was swollen."

"And..." Maggie said with a laugh.

"He dropped a favor, and we both reached for it at the same time, and then we kissed. It was...amazing. Unfortunately, the cuckoo clock went off, which was like throwing a bucket of ice water on a fire. But it turned out to be a good thing, because I am way too busy for dating, and we have to share a building, and he's my landlord—"

"Stop, Kate," Maggie said. "You are making too many excuses. If the kiss was amazing, why didn't you get back to it?"

"Because my brain started working again, and I remembered all the things I just said."

"It's not like you work for him," Jessica put in.

"No, but he and I are not on the same page when it comes to love and romance. Barrett is very cynical. He's divorced. He hates weddings. He thinks big weddings lead to big marriage problems. Everything I do seems like a joke to him. I mean, seriously, there is no way we could have any kind of relationship."

"He hates weddings, but he helped you make favors?" Jessica gave her a perplexed look. "That says something—like he's interested in you."

"I don't think it says that. He was just trying to ward off a lawsuit."

"That's not even close to being true, and you know it," Maggie said.

"You like him," Jessica added, with a gleam in her eyes. "That's a good thing, Kate. You haven't liked anyone in a while."

"I think it's bad, very bad," she said with a sigh, not bothering to continue trying to deny the truth to two of her best friends.

"It's not bad," Maggie said. "When's the last time

you had a boyfriend?"

"I don't know. I'm busy."

"It's not about being busy; it's about taking a risk. You like to play it safe."

"I take risks," she said defensively. "I've risked everything on my business."

"But you don't risk your heart," Jessica said, giving her an understanding smile. "And I get it. I was really battered after my first disastrous marriage. I didn't think I could ever get married again, but then I met Reid, and everything changed. I knew he was worth it. Love isn't something to be missed. You, of all people, should know that. You're the most romantic one of all of us."

"That's not really true," Maggie muttered. "About Kate being the most romantic."

"You don't think I'm romantic?" she asked in surprise.

"I think you're romantic for everyone else, but for yourself...not so much. Why don't you ask this Barrett Fox out for a drink? Thank him for helping you with the favors," Maggie continued.

"No way. I already thanked him, and I fed him pizza. That's all he gets." She picked up her menu. "Now, let's order and then we'll get down to business."

As much as she'd been reluctant to see Barrett again, Kate was a little annoyed when Wednesday came around, and she realized it had been five days since she'd seen him. She'd heard his voice a few times when he'd walked a client out the door, but that was about it. He'd made no attempt to come upstairs, and every time she'd entered the building, she'd rushed up to her office, trying not to glance at his door, trying not to think about him, trying not to wonder about the kiss she wished they'd kept going.

Pressing her fingers to her temples, she realized she'd drifted off in the middle of a meeting, but her client had been going on and on for a good ten minutes, about pretty much nothing. Jana Davis was a twenty-three-year-old spoiled rich girl, who had been referred by another one of her brides, but so far couldn't seem to find anything she liked, whether it was flowers or cakes or music. She also couldn't pick a wedding venue, even though they'd toured several locations twice already. They were getting nowhere fast, because Jana couldn't decide on anything. Her latest ramble was basically a stream of consciousness monologue about what she might want or not want.

"I just don't know if the winery in Napa is right, Kate," Jana said more loudly. "What if some people don't want to travel? But then, the Vicksham Manor is a little dark and I didn't care for their menu. My mother wants me to do it in Hawaii, but if people won't go to Napa, will they go to Maui? I don't know what to do. Tell me what I should pick."

"I can't tell you. It has to be your choice. We can go over all the pros and cons again," she said, forcing back the urge to scream in frustration. They'd already gone over that list three times.

"Maybe I should have gone with a bigger wedding planning service, one who has florists and caterers on staff."

"I can get you anything you want," she said, realizing that Jana was now taking out her frustration on her.

Jana crossed her arms and tapped her foot impatiently on the floor. "You couldn't get me into the Palmer Hotel."

"They're booked years in advance."

"If you had clout, you could have gotten me in."

"The room at the Palmer is out of your budget, Jana, even if it was available."

"My mother can cough up more money. She can take it out of her facelift fund." Jana paused as loud voices rang through the air. "What is that about?"

"Those people must be going to the office downstairs." She got up from her desk. "Let me shut the door."

When she reached the doorway, a string of obscene swearwords floated up the stairway.

"What is happening?" Jana demanded, following her into the outer office. "Is that another bridal couple?"

"I seriously doubt it. They are probably visiting the attorney downstairs. He specializes in divorce law."

"Well, we can't continue our meeting with all this noise."

She frowned. Shari had gone home for the day, so she couldn't send her downstairs to shut things down. *Where the hell was Barrett? Why wasn't he dealing with his clients?*

As more sexual insults rang out, she said, "Let me just tell those two to take their argument elsewhere."

She marched down the stairs, her annoyance turning to fury as Barrett stood in the doorway to his office, listening to the man and woman vent their anger.

"What on earth is going on?" she demanded,

stopping halfway down the stairs.

"They're having a minor disagreement," he shouted back, running one hand through his hair in agitation.

"Well, do something," she ordered.

He turned back to the arguing couple, who were standing no more than six inches from each other but were yelling at the top of their lungs. "Gary—Janice. Please, calm down."

They both ignored him, and he threw up his hands in disgust. "See what I mean?"

Kate took a deep breath, furious at the disruption. She stomped back up the stairs and into her office only to run into Jana, who was obviously on her way out.

Kate tried to apologize, but Jana was not about to be placated. "This is totally unprofessional," she said angrily. "I'll expect my deposit back in the morning."

"Please, this is a very unusual occurrence. Why don't we meet at your home tomorrow? Then we can avoid any other unfortunate situations."

Jana hesitated, still plainly irritated by the events. "All right. But you'll have to call me for an appointment. I don't have my date book with me, and I'm not sure I'm free tomorrow. This is really inconvenient, Kate."

"I agree, and I'm sorry. I'll call you tomorrow," she said hastily, as Jana left the office. While she wouldn't really mind losing Jana's business, her bank account would miss her large deposit, and she'd already spent a lot of time on Jana's wedding. She needed to salvage things.

But first...she was going to end the scene going on downstairs.

As she spied the water pitcher on the table, a really bad idea came into her head, but she was just that annoyed.

She grabbed the pitcher. It was only a quarter full, but that should be enough to get someone's attention. She walked down the stairs and noticed that Barrett was nowhere in sight. *The coward.* He had probably gone home and left those two to destroy the building.

"Excuse me," she called out loudly.

"Stay out of this," the woman shouted, without missing a beat in her continuing tirade.

"Look, this has got to stop," she said. "This is a place of business." Neither one paid any attention to her, and Kate's irritation turned to full-blown fury when the woman grabbed the large brass coatrack at the bottom of the stairs and pushed it over, narrowly missing her opponent. Without further thought, Kate raised her arm and tossed the water into their faces.

Time stood still as two dripping faces looked at her in confusion, and the resulting silence was deafening. Kate eyed them warily, wondering if she had gone too far.

"Well, well, well." Barrett clapped his hands as he came through the door. "Very nice, Kate."

"This is outrageous, Mr. Fox," the woman said, finally getting her voice back. "This is a five-hundred-dollar dress." She glanced down at the rumpled silk in complete dismay.

"No, your behavior is outrageous," Barrett replied angrily. "I have just called the police, and they should be here at any moment to see that the two of you conduct your argument elsewhere."

The woman's mouth dropped open at his statement. "But Barrett, he started it."

"I don't care. And I won't be representing either one of you."

"But you're the best," she said. "Give me another chance."

"I'm sorry, no. Please go."

"He's right, we should go," the man said, looking at Barrett's stony expression and then at Kate's angry face. "I don't want this to get into the papers."

"You and your publicity, that's all you care about," the woman said angrily.

Kate sighed. It looked like the water was only a temporary setback. They were ready to start the second round. But before they could say anything further, Barrett opened the front door and literally pushed them both onto the doorstep, slamming the door behind them, and turning the dead bolt with a resounding click.

He turned around with a guarded expression on his face, and she gave him an uncertain look. She didn't know what to expect. Thoughts of possible eviction sprang to mind as she shifted back and forth nervously, hoping he would speak first because she couldn't think of a thing to say.

"I'm sorry about that, Kate. I had no idea they were going to get involved in such a violent argument."

She let out a relief at his apology. "They might have lost me a client."

His lips tightened at her pointed remark. "I hope the words *might have* mean you'll be able to smooth things over."

"We'll see. Those two were really nasty to each other. Does this happen a lot in your line of work?"

"It really doesn't. I was just in initial talks with

the wife. But, apparently, her husband insisted on following her here and their argument started before they ever got into the building. The woman just found out her husband has had a lover for the past five years, who is now pregnant. Naturally she's a little upset."

"A little upset? If I were him, I wouldn't turn my back on her. She wants to kill him."

"She told me their entire relationship has been volatile."

"I don't know how you deal with all that anger."

"It's not usually that violent or that verbal." He paused as the doorbell rang. "That's probably the police." He opened the door to two uniformed officers standing on the landing.

"We got a call about a disturbance," one officer said, taking a good look at Kate and then at Barrett. "Is there a problem here?"

"No, the problem just left," Barrett replied.

"Are you all right, miss?" the other officer asked, directing his comment to Kate.

She looked at him in surprise. He thought she and Barrett were the ones who had been fighting. "I'm fine. The two people who were arguing just left."

The officer stared at them thoughtfully, his gaze drifting to her splinted fingers. "If you're sure."

"I'm sure," she answered.

"I'm the one who called you," Barrett said with annoyance.

"Okay. Have a good night."

Barrett shut the door and shook his head. "What a day."

"You can say that again," she said, rubbing her aching temple once more. "I thought I had it bad with Jana but compared to your clients, she's a delight.

Why do you do it, Barrett? Why this kind of law?"

"Because people going through a divorce need help. They're too emotional to take a step back and divide up their property equally. They need an objective observer who can help make things fair."

"I guess."

"I see you got a splint for your fingers. Are they broken?"

"No, just jammed. They're already feeling a lot better. I can probably get rid of the splint now."

"I'm glad. I was wondering."

She wanted to be touched by his comment, but his wondering certainly hadn't led him to make a short trip up the stairs to find out if she was all right.

"Are you finished for the day?" he asked.

"I guess I am. Jana was my last client."

"Then I'd like to take you to dinner—as an apology for possibly losing you a client."

"If you knew the size of her deposit, you'd be offering a private plane ride to Paris for dinner."

He smiled. "How about an Italian restaurant in North Beach?"

She hesitated, her first instinct to say no, to keep her guard walls up, but maybe she needed to spend more time with Barrett, to remind herself that he was not someone she needed to waste her time thinking about. It was just dinner.

Nothing else had to happen.

"It's good," Barrett added. "What do you say?"

She should say no, she meant to say no, but when he looked at her with those intense green eyes and that sexy smile, the only thing she wanted to say was yes, and before she knew it, she was comfortably ensconced in a silver-gray Mercedes.

Chapter Seven

——➤➤➤◄◄◄◄——

As Barrett drove into North Beach, famous for its excellent Italian cuisine, Kate's mouth began to water at the sight of famous restaurants like Original Joe's and Mama's, but when Barrett helped her out of the car, they didn't head toward one of the known hot spots. Instead, he walked her toward a long, dark alley.

"Where are we going?" she asked.

"You'll see." He took her hand. "So you don't trip in those high heels. I don't think you need another fall."

She definitely didn't need that, but that wasn't the real reason she left her hand in his. His fingers were warm, and she liked feeling connected to him. She liked him. She hadn't wanted to admit that to her friends, but she had to admit it to herself.

But as soon as this dinner was over, she had to start putting some distance between them, because her reasons for staying away from him were still there.

Barrett led her down a stairwell to a closed door. The only sign for the restaurant was a simple gold placard—*Sonny's*.

"I've never heard of this place," she said.

"You're going to love it. One of San Francisco's best-kept secrets." He opened the door and waved her inside.

She let go of his hand as she stepped across the threshold. She paused, as her eyes adjusted to the dim light. There was a hostess stand in front of thick red curtains, and beyond, she could see about twenty tables in front of an open kitchen.

Barrett gave his name to the hostess, and they were quickly led to a cozy corner booth that faced the kitchen but was away from the noise. Soft strains of opera played in the background, and several small candles floating in a bowl of water cast their table in a warm, romantic glow.

She was surprised at Barrett's choice. She would have thought something glitzy, more modern would be his style.

"This is nice," she said. "When did you make a reservation?"

"I texted when we got in the car. The owner is a friend of mine."

After the waiter dropped off the wine list and announced the specials, a very short, round man with a thick moustache greeted Barrett in effusive Italian.

She was more than a little surprised when Barrett responded in kind.

Then he turned to her with a grin. "Don't be too impressed. My Italian is limited to a few greetings, a couple of swear words, and—"

"The words of amore," Sonny finished for him.

"Who is this lovely lady?"

"This is Kate Marlow," Barrett introduced. "My good friend, Sonny Moretti."

Sonny took her hand and kissed it with a flourish. "I am pleased to meet you, Miss Marlow. For you and my good friend, Barrett, I will make the finest dinner. You leave it up to me, yes?"

Barrett looked expectantly at Kate and she nodded. "I'm sure whatever you make will be wonderful."

"It will be," Sonny promised. "It's been a long time since you've come to visit me, Barrett. I thought perhaps you had developed a taste for something finer."

Barrett shook his head. "There is nothing finer than your pasta."

Sonny beamed at his response. "For that, I will also send over a bottle of my best wine."

Kate smiled to herself as Sonny gathered up their menus. Barrett certainly had a charming side to him.

"What's so amusing?" he asked.

"Just thinking that you can be very nice when you want to be. You have a way with words—in more than one language apparently."

"I'm a lawyer. Words are my business."

"Right. I almost forgot."

"I'm really not that bad, you know. I help people salvage as much as they can out of their marriage."

"It all comes down to money and possessions," she said with a sigh.

"Not just material things," he argued. "There's also pride and self-respect, mutual understanding, finding a way to keep a family working together in a divorced world."

She was surprised by his passionate, somewhat emotional words. It really wasn't just about money for him. He cared about his work, about the people he served. "All that is important," she conceded. "Although, I think the kids suffer no matter what."

"I can't stop that. But I can try to ease the pain."

"If the parties are willing to compromise. The couple outside your office tonight didn't seem able to do anything but argue. Do they have children?"

"A fifteen-year-old daughter. I'm trying to get them to put her first, but they're caught up in anger and bitterness. Hopefully, that will start to fade at some point."

"I doubt that will happen any time soon." She paused, as the waiter opened a bottle of wine and poured a sample taste.

"You go ahead," Barrett told her.

"I'm sure you're more of a wine connoisseur than I am."

"I trust your judgment."

"Okay." She tasted the wine and nodded to the waiter. "It's lovely."

The waiter poured them two glasses and then left them alone.

"What happened in your marriage?" she asked, not sure Barrett would answer. "If you don't mind me asking."

He hesitated, then shrugged. "It's not a secret. Vanessa wanted the big wedding, but once all the hoopla was over, she didn't know what to do with herself. She also apparently didn't realize that while I was part of the Fox family, I wasn't interested in living their life. I didn't care about the country club, the golf games or tennis matches. I didn't want to go to social events every weekend. I didn't want every conversation to be about who was cheating on who or who had the most money."

"And you didn't realize that's what she wanted before you got married? Was she the only one who made incorrect assumptions?"

He tipped his head at her point. "No, of course not. We both saw what we wanted to see, and we didn't ask too many questions or look past the wedding."

"Did Vanessa work?"

"Yes. She worked for an interior designer, who handled a lot of rich and celebrity clients. The job put her in the world she wanted to be in, but also again required me to be in that world with her."

"Why didn't you want to be a part of it?" she asked curiously. "You grew up in that environment. And there are a lot of perks. I'm not going to feel sorry for you because you had to play tennis at the country club."

He smiled. "Fair enough. And you shouldn't feel sorry for me. I was fortunate to have everything I needed. But life isn't just about material things. It took me awhile to realize that."

"How long were you together before you got married?"

"About a year and a half."

"That's not very long."

"I wasn't thinking straight."

"She was that pretty?"

"She was—is—quite beautiful," he admitted. "But the pretty was only on the outside. Once we started planning our wedding, I began to see another side to her. She would have meltdowns over menu choices and flower arrangements. Nothing was good enough or special enough or unique enough. She was obsessed. She lived and breathed the wedding plans. And her planner cheered her on at every turn. It was more, more, more."

"The wedding planner was trying to give her what she wanted."

"But not what I wanted."

"Did you tell anyone what you wanted?" she challenged. "Communication is a two-way street. I always talk to the grooms, and I make a point of speaking to them when their brides are not around, so that I can make sure the day works for them, too. However, most men tend to leave the decisions up to the woman. Sometimes you get what you get because you don't speak up."

"I should have spoken up more," he conceded.

"And I don't think you can blame the wedding for all your problems. It sounds like you were on different pages when it came to what you wanted from your life together."

"I don't blame the wedding, but I think it set an unrealistic expectation that we couldn't possibly live up to."

She rested her arms on the table as she thought about his statement. "Do you think that if you'd gotten married at the courthouse, you would still be married today?"

He frowned. "Maybe you should have been an attorney. You're very good at debate, picking apart arguments."

"And you're good at avoiding a question you don't want to answer."

He tipped his head. "No. I don't think we'd still be

married today."

She felt like she'd won a small victory. "I don't think so, either. What's Vanessa doing today?"

"My mother told me a few weeks ago that she's engaged to be married to an architect. I'm sure she's planning the hell out of another wedding."

"Would you get married again, Barrett?"

"I can't imagine it. I don't think I'm husband material." He paused. "What about you? I know you haven't been married, but have you come close? Are you involved with anyone now?"

"I'm not seeing anyone at the moment, and I haven't come close to an engagement. I haven't met anyone I want to spend the next sixty years with."

"I'd start with six months and go from there."

"I'm not going to get married unless I believe we can go the distance."

"How would you know?" he asked curiously. "There are so many pretenses played out in the dating world—so many games, masks that are worn, double talk—how can you really be sure who that person is?"

"By having really honest and sometimes difficult conversations. By seeing each other at your worst and at your best. By prioritizing what's important."

"What's important to you?"

"Having someone I can count on, who will be there when I fall, who will be my partner through life. I want honesty and trust."

"What about passion, sex?"

Her cheeks warmed at his words and at the look of desire in his eyes. "Well, chemistry is also important. But it can't be everything."

"It can be a lot."

"Or too much. Sometimes, when the attraction is

so strong, it stops a person from seeing what's not there outside of the physical relationship." She paused. "I'm sure some of your clients must have expressed that sentiment."

"A few. I'll be honest, Kate. I don't know much about love, not the kind of love you're talking about. I haven't seen it in my family. I haven't seen it in my work."

"Well, you should meet my grandparents."

"You think they'd set me straight?" he asked with a grin.

"Definitely." She licked her lips. "What you just said, though, is why you and I do not go together."

"You wouldn't think so," he said cryptically. "But you do look beautiful in candlelight, Kate."

A shiver ran down her spine at the look in his eyes. "Everyone looks better in candlelight."

"A better answer would be *thank you*," he said lightly, a smile lurking around the corners of his mouth. "Or you could say I look good, too."

"I'll stick with thank you," she said, trying to quell the nervous flutters in her stomach.

Thankfully, the waiter came by with hot bread out of the oven and a plate of olive oil mixed with balsamic vinegar.

"The bread is amazing," Barrett told her, as he grabbed a hunk and dipped it in the olive oil.

She followed suit and had to admit he was right again. "Delicious," she agreed. "I love warm bread fresh out of the oven."

"Nothing better. Although, I did realize on our way over here that we had pizza last night, so it's a double dose of Italian for you."

"I love Italian. How could I not, living so close to

North Beach? And I'm very intrigued in San Francisco's best-kept secret."

"I don't think you'll be disappointed."

"I'm sure I won't be." She'd no sooner finished speaking when Sonny accompanied the waiter to their table, delivering a large salad to share, along with two steaming plates of pasta and vegetables covered with a garlic parmesan sauce.

"Enjoy," Sonny said.

"I definitely will," she promised, immediately twirling long strands of linguine on her fork, and popping the first delicious bite into her mouth. "Oh, my God. This is fantastic."

Barrett smiled. "I thought you'd like it."

They didn't talk for a while, content to eat in comfortable silence. When they did speak, it was about light, inconsequential things such as movies, books, and the city. They found to their mutual surprise that they did actually have a few things in common. They both liked reading mysteries and sailing on the bay, as well as eating lobster tails on Fisherman's Wharf.

Of course, they also had their differences. Barrett didn't share her love of cable cars, preferring to drive, instead of taking a steep, slow ride up a hill. She didn't share his love of running along the Marina out to the Golden Gate Bridge. And the bicycle she rode was in a spin class at the gym, while Barrett preferred the long winding trails down the coast.

"I'm beginning to realize you're quite the outdoorsman," she commented, as they sipped coffee and nibbled on both tiramisu and cannolis.

"I like to eat, so I need to work it off."

"Which you like to do outside."

"We live in California. We should take advantage of the great weather."

"I like the weather. I just enjoy looking at the bay from a boat or a restaurant with a view." She paused. "Speaking of restaurants, this place is really special. I'm glad you brought me here."

"Happy to share it with you. But I have to say, you're not a very considerate dinner partner. Most of the women I know leave half their plate for me to finish."

She grinned at his teasing comment. "Not me. I also love food, as you can probably tell."

"You can have the last cannoli."

"I couldn't possibly. I'm stuffed. Go ahead."

"I think I'm done." He pushed his dessert plate away and rested his arms on the table. "This was nice. We can apparently get along without arguing."

"We seem to do better outside the office. I guess it's easier for us to forget that what we each do for a living contradicts the other."

"I don't know. We're just working on different ends of a life experience, that's all." He stopped abruptly, sitting back in his chair, as a stunning redhead walked over to the table. "Vanessa," he murmured.

Vanessa? His ex-wife Vanessa?

Chapter Eight

—➤➤➤◀◀◀—

"It's been awhile," Vanessa said, as Barrett rose to his feet, looking more than a little uncomfortable.

"It has," he agreed.

"I should have figured I'd run into you here. It's your favorite place."

"And I never thought I'd run into you here," Barrett replied shortly. "You were never a fan of Sonny's."

"A client of mine is having a birthday party in the private room."

He nodded, his jaw tight. "Okay."

"How have you been?" Vanessa asked.

"Great." He didn't bother to ask how she had been.

As Kate watched the two of them give each other a long, tense look, she wondered if there was any love still between them or if it was anger that put the crackle in the air.

Barrett seemed like he'd completely forgotten she

was there, and the model-pretty redhead hadn't even bothered to acknowledge her.

"We should talk sometime," Vanessa said. "I have been thinking about you lately. My father is having a retirement party next week. He mentioned he wouldn't mind seeing you there."

"I don't think so," Barrett said.

"You used to like my dad."

He shrugged.

"It wasn't all bad, Barrett," she continued.

"I think you've forgotten a lot."

"Or maybe you have. You look good." Her gaze ran down his fit, handsome body.

"So do you," he muttered.

As another awkward pause dropped between them, Kate cleared her throat.

Barrett started, giving her a quick glance. "Sorry. This is Vanessa—Richards," he said, stumbling over the last name. "You went back to your maiden name, didn't you?"

"I did," she said shortly.

"This is Kate Marlow."

"Hello," she said.

Vanessa gave her a nod and a quick, "Hello." Then she said, "I need to meet my client. Think about the party, Barrett. It's a week from Friday. It would mean a lot to my father."

"I doubt your fiancé would appreciate my presence."

"Oh." Her expression changed, a bleak look entering her eyes. "There is no fiancé, not anymore. This one was smart enough to bail before the wedding," she said with a touch of sarcasm. "My father's party is at Rutherford's Steak House, seven thirty."

"I'm sorry, but I can't make it."

She sighed. "All right. I'll let him know."

As Vanessa moved away, Barrett sat down, his jaw still tight, dark shadows in his eyes.

"So, that's your ex," she murmured.

"I can't believe she came here. She always hated this place. She wanted to go to restaurants where she could be seen."

"She's very attractive." She licked her lips. "Any lingering feelings?"

"God, no." Anger tightened his lips. "Why would you ask me that?"

"That was a very tense conversation. You two were caught up in each other. You forgot I was even here."

"I didn't forget. I was just surprised to see her, that's all. There's nothing left between us."

"She wants you to come to her father's party. She looked at you like she'd forgotten how attractive you are."

He frowned. "If she wants me to come to that party, it's because she needs me for something. Vanessa is a user. She's your best friend when she wants something. It took me too long to figure that out, but I won't forget it. Our relationship has been over for three years. There's nothing left. I'm sorry if you felt left out—"

"I didn't feel left out," she interrupted. "I was just curious. That was one of the most awkward conversations I've witnessed in a while."

He blew out an angry breath. "I apologize for that. Vanessa never brought out the best in me, and that's apparently still the case. To be fair, I didn't bring out the best in her, either. We looked good on paper. Everyone said we were perfect together. Our families liked each other. In fact, my mother adored Vanessa. Vanessa was going to be the daughter she never had. But while Vanessa might have fit into my family better than I did, she did not fit with me. Or maybe I'm just not a man who should be married. I'm just glad we broke it up before we had a kid."

She inwardly flinched as his words reminded her of her past. "That was good. Bringing a kid into a terrible situation is never a smart idea."

His gaze filled with apology. "I'm sorry, Kate. I hit a nerve, didn't I?"

"It's fine. You and my father are not the same person."

"Definitely not. I wouldn't have walked away from my child, no matter how I felt about Vanessa. I don't have any respect for men who walk away from their kids. I dropped a client last month because he wanted to get out of paying child support."

"Really?"

"Yes," he said, holding her gaze. "The kid deserved better."

"I'm glad you stood up for what you believed in."

"I always do. I think you do, too."

"Most of the time. I bend a lot when it comes to brides, but I try not to cross any lines I shouldn't cross. At the end of the day, I have to be proud of what I do. It's not always easy, though. Sometimes I need money to make rent and pay bills. It's a juggling act."

"Which you seem to do well, even with one hand in a splint." He paused. "By the way, how did your friends like the favors?"

"They loved them and were sure their guys

would, too."

"Are these friends from childhood?"

"No, they're from college. My freshman year in the dorms, I got into a group of girls, and we became very close, very tight friends. After graduation, we vowed that no matter where we were in life, we'd come back and stand up for each other. There are eight of us in the group, and Jessica and Maggie will be the sixth and seventh brides to get married in the past few years. It's been a crazy time."

"So, wait a second. Does that mean you're the only single woman left?"

She made a face at him. "Yes, and that's a fact everyone loves to point out to me. But I don't care. It's not a race to the finish, and I don't feel like an old maid yet. Maybe in a few years."

He smiled. "I don't see you as an old maid, not with your romantic view of life. Have you planned all the weddings?"

"Every single one, but this next one is a double wedding, and I've never done that before. I want to make sure that both Jess and Maggie feel like it's their special day. It's especially important because Jessica had a very short, very bad marriage when we were seniors in college. She got pregnant and she and her boyfriend decided to do the right thing and get married, but they weren't really in love, and her boyfriend quickly realized that he also didn't want to be a husband or a father, so Jess ended up a single mom. And before you try to blame the wedding, she got married in a courthouse, with about ten people there."

"I didn't say every divorce was because of the wedding."

"This one definitely wasn't. Anyway, for a long time, Jessica didn't feel like she deserved a second chance, nor did she have time to fall in love. She had a son to take care of. But last year she met Reid, and he swept her off her feet, almost literally. He's a fireman. He had to rescue her from a doghouse."

"That sounds like a story."

"I don't know all the details, but her son called 911 when he realized his mother was stuck, and that's how they met. Jessica is a teacher in Half Moon Bay. She and Reid are moving into a pretty new house on the coast after the wedding."

"What about Maggie? What's her story? How did she meet her fiancé?" he asked with interest.

"She was working for a hotel in Napa, the Stratton, when a really grungy guy came in, and her manager insisted she give him the worst room in the house. He didn't want that kind of guest in the hotel. Maggie was reluctant to follow through, which was a good thing, because the guest was undercover. Cole was, in fact, the owner's nephew, and he was there to see how the hotel was operating. Maggie and Cole ended up falling in love, and they recently bought an old inn that is part of a winery in Napa. They're refurbishing it together."

"Another great story. Who else is in the group?"

"This cannot be interesting for you."

"On the contrary, I'm intrigued."

"Well, there's Andrea and her twin sister, Laurel. Laurel was the first to get married. She and Greg were high school sweethearts. Then her sister, Andrea, met Alexander Donovan, the billionaire toy and game maker, when she was sent to interview him. They fell in love and got married. Julie married a baseball player, Matt Kingsley."

"Wait, I know that name. He plays for the Cougars. He's a superstar."

"Not just in baseball, also in life. Julie was really reluctant to fall in love with him, because her father was also an amazing ballplayer but a not-so-great husband and father. She was afraid Matt would be the same, but he's not. Julie actually runs Matt's charitable foundation. And then there's Liz and Michael. They knew each other in high school and then fell in love when they were competing for some PR business. Michael Stafford was a pro football player, but he got injured and went into the PR business with his sister. But that didn't last too long. He's a coach at Stanford now."

"I don't follow football as much as baseball," Barrett commented.

"Last but not least is Isabella. She's a dance teacher and Nick is in the hotel business. They met when he had to learn the tango to impress an Argentinian investor."

Barrett laughed. "Come on. Seriously?"

"No lie. And Isabella said he was not the best student. But they fell in love."

"You have quite a crew."

"And it's getting bigger. Andrea and Liz both have kids now and Julie is expecting."

"Everyone lives close by?"

"Within a few hours."

"You're lucky."

"Really lucky," she agreed. "They're the best friends in the world, even aside from all the wedding mania. They're the kind of people who are there for you when you need them. I'm sure you have friends like that."

"Not quite so many, but I have a couple of friends from college and a few more from law school who I stay in touch with."

"Have you always worked in your own law office?"

"No. I started out in a big firm doing corporate law, working a million hours a week. lasted about four years." He paused. "Vanessa's father was a partner at that firm. That's how Vanessa and I met actually—at a company party."

"Oh. Now I understand why she'd think you'd be interested in going to her father's retirement party."

"He was a mentor to me. I liked him very much. In the end, I probably liked him more than I did Vanessa."

"Did you leave the firm because of your divorce?"

"No, I left six months before we separated. I was tired of what I was doing, and I had an offer to work in family law. I liked the idea of doing something more personal. But taking that job was a step back, not a step forward in terms of money and stature, and Vanessa was not happy about it. She didn't understand why I couldn't be happy doing the same job her father had been doing for years. It was probably close to the final straw."

"Well, you should do what you're passionate about. And as your wife, she should have supported you."

"I thought so, too."

"It was your job, not hers."

"Exactly. But my salary went down, the people I was working with changed, and she felt like I'd changed, which I had. I was finally being true to myself. Now, I run my own firm, and for the most part, my clients are great. Tonight's incident was an exception."

"I hope so." She looked up as Sonny came over to the table.

"How did you like your food?" Sonny asked.

"It was fantastic," she answered. "The best pasta I've ever had."

"Thank you," Sonny said, beaming with pleasure at her words.

"It was great, as always," Barrett added. "And I want to see the bill this time."

"Never. At Sonny's, you always eat for free." Sonny glanced back at Kate. "Did Barrett tell you what he did for me?"

"No, he didn't."

"You don't need to get into that old story," Barrett protested.

"He saved my life," Sonny said.

"He's exaggerating," Barrett cut in.

"Not even a little bit," Sonny said, with a shake of his head.

"Well, tell me the story," she urged.

"My wife, Theresa, hired Barrett to be her divorce attorney. We were having trouble in our marriage about three years ago, but I didn't really know what had changed, why my wife was so distant. Barrett convinced Theresa to share a painful, personal secret she'd been carrying around for a long time. It was a secret she couldn't bear for me to find out, so she thought she'd divorce me before that could happen. But Barrett urged her to talk to me about it. We worked things out and found our way back to each other. Of course, Barrett lost her business, so I try to make it up to him in free meals."

"I've told you before, there's nothing to be made up," Barrett said.

"I'm glad you got your wife back," she said.

Sonny gave her a smile. "I have a feeling you want to know what the secret was."

"I would never ask you that," she replied, although she was very curious.

"It's not a secret anymore. My stepbrother made a move on Theresa when she had too much wine one night. She'd been drinking a lot that week. Her mother had passed on, and she was struggling. My stepbrother took photos of her passed out on a bed, making it look like they'd slept together. Then he blackmailed her. He wanted me to invest in his business, and I had already said no. After Theresa told me what was happening, I was furious—at both of them, if I'm being honest. But when I really listened to Theresa, I started to understand that the situation was more complicated. I hadn't understood that she'd started drinking not only because she was missing her mother but also because she was lonely. I was here at the restaurant every night. I had put work before my marriage." Sonny glanced at Barrett. "If Theresa and I hadn't listened to Barrett, we might be divorced now."

"You're giving me too much credit," Barrett said. "I just got you in the room together. You and Theresa did the rest."

"You have no idea how difficult it was for us to talk to each other," Sonny said, giving Barrett a grateful smile. "Anyway, it's all good now. Communication is the key. You two should remember that."

At his curious glance, she immediately shook her head. "We're not together like that. We're just...friends."

"What she said," Barrett added as Sonny's gaze moved to him. "We share office space. That's it."

"All right. I'll leave it alone," Sonny said with amusement. "But if I could give you both just a little advice—life is shorter than you think. Don't waste a second. Now, I must see to the other diners. Please come back soon."

"You certainly have a devoted fan," she said to Barrett as Sonny left.

"I really didn't do that much. I tell people to talk all the time. Most of them don't. Luckily, Sonny and Theresa did."

She nodded, thinking Barrett had a lot more depth than she'd first thought. "Do you wish you'd tried to talk more honestly with Vanessa?"

"I wish I'd done a lot of things differently. But it's all in the past. I can't change it, so I move on."

"Next time, you'll do it differently."

He frowned. "I told you. There isn't going to be a next time."

"Everyone says that and then they meet the right person, and it changes. One mistake doesn't have to mean you're done with love for life."

"I can have love without marriage."

"Can you?" she countered. "Real love that lasts forever? I think marriage makes a difference. My mother said she was so in love with my father that she didn't feel she needed a piece of paper. But as soon as something happened that my father didn't like, like my birth, he took off."

"He probably would have done the same even if

he was married to your mother."

"Or maybe he would have tried a little harder for a little longer."

His gaze softened. "You can't blame yourself for breaking them up. You were a baby."

"I don't blame myself. I blame him. Actually, I blame both of them for not figuring out what they really wanted before they conceived me."

"People in love can be impulsive and reckless."

"I know. But it's not an excuse."

"It sounds to me like you're going to want a guarantee before you go down the aisle."

"Not a guarantee, just someone willing to commit to me in front of my family and friends. And, yes, I know I could still end up in divorce. But I feel like I have a better chance of beating those odds if I make sure I've found the right person, someone who wants what I want."

"And that hasn't happened yet."

"Not yet, but when it's right, it will be right."

"What if you fall in love with someone who doesn't want to get married?"

"I don't think I could," she murmured, although as she studied Barrett's handsome face in the candlelight, she had a feeling she was lying to herself. "I want everything: the engagement, the wedding, the marriage, the happily ever after. And I think I deserve it."

He stared back at her, his gaze unreadable. "If that's what you want, it's what you should have."

She didn't know how their conversation had gotten so deep so fast. Barrett had just built a pretty solid wall between them, reminding her that he did not want what she wanted. She needed to tamp down the attraction she was feeling toward him. He might be sexy as hell, with lips she really wanted to kiss, but she couldn't go down that road.

"We should go," she said. "It's getting crowded, and I'm sure Sonny would like the table."

"Right," he said, glancing around the room. "I didn't realize all the tables had filled up."

She grabbed her bag and Barrett led her out of the restaurant.

As they hit the street, she pulled her coat more tightly around her shoulders. Fog had descended on San Francisco, and it was a cold, wintry night. As they walked down the dark alley, Barrett took her hand in his, and a searing warmth ran through her. She wanted to hang on to that heat, but she had a feeling if she did, she could get burned.

Barrett was feeling way too many emotions as he slid behind the wheel. Letting go of Kate's hand had been far more difficult than it should have been. They'd just had a very clear-cut conversation that showed how different they thought about love and marriage. She was not someone he needed to mess around with and vice versa.

He just wished he wasn't so attracted to her, that he didn't like her passion and fire so much, that he didn't respect the fact that she knew what she wanted and she wasn't about to settle for anything less, that he didn't feel like he wanted to rise to the challenge she'd just laid down—that she couldn't fall for someone who didn't want to get married.

He knew she could feel the heat between them.

She was just determined to fight it.

He should do the same. That would be the smart thing to do.

"My car is at the office," Kate said suddenly, breaking into his reverie. "You can just take me back there."

"Of course." Maybe it was better he wouldn't be taking her home, wouldn't be tempted to see if he could get himself invited inside.

Kate's phone buzzed, and she reached for it. "I'm sorry. I have to take this. It's my grandfather."

"No problem."

"Grandpa?" she said. "Is everything okay? What? Is she all right?"

He could hear a man's agitated voice on the line.

"Wait. Where are you?" Kate asked, then paused. "I'll come right away. It's going to be okay." She listened for another moment. "Don't think that way. Grandma is strong. She's a fighter. I'll be there as soon as I can."

"What's wrong?" he asked.

She looked at him with fear in her eyes. "My grandparents were in a car accident. My grandmother is hurt, and it sounds serious. I have to get to the hospital."

"I'll take you."

"They're in Oakland. I have to get my car. Oh, God, Barrett, what if…"

"Don't think that way," he said, repeating what she'd just told her grandfather. He made a U-turn at the next intersection, heading toward the Bay Bridge.

"You don't have to drive me."

"It's not a big deal. It will take longer for us to get back to your car."

"All right. Thank you," she said, twisting her fingers together. "I've been telling them both that they need to stop driving. I even put apps on their phones, so they could get rides, but they've always insisted that they don't go far, that they're fine." She looked over at him as he came to a light. "My grandmother raised me. My grandfather was the dad I never had. I love them so much. I can't lose either one of them. I just can't."

"I really hope you won't," he said heavily.

Chapter Nine

They found Kate's grandfather in the waiting room adjacent to the surgical center. He was a tall, thin, balding man who had a bandage on his head and looked pale and shaky as Kate embraced him. Barrett stood off to the side, not wanting to get in the way.

"How's Grandma?" Kate asked.

"She's in surgery," her grandfather replied. "They said there's internal bleeding. They're trying to stop it."

"How are you?" she asked, her gaze narrowing on the bandage on his temple. "Did you hit your head?"

"I'm fine. They checked me out. I just got a cut from some flying glass."

"What happened?"

"A car ran a red light." His gaze hardened with anger. "Damn red-light runner. It wasn't my fault, Katie. I had the green light. Witnesses said so. The kid came out of nowhere. And he hopped out without a scratch." He shook his head. "But maybe I should have taken another look or waited a second longer to enter the intersection."

She put a hand on her grandfather's arm. "Don't blame yourself. It sounds like you were completely in the right."

"Being right doesn't get your grandmother out of surgery."

"Being wrong won't do that, either. She's going to be all right. She has to be."

The older man nodded. "I can't live without her. She's my rock."

"I know."

Her grandfather's gaze moved past Kate, settling on him. "Who are you?"

Kate started. "Oh, sorry, Grandpa. This is Barrett Fox. He was driving me home from dinner when you called, so he brought me here." She turned to him. "This is my grandfather, Lance Harding."

"Sir," he said, shaking the man's hand. "I'm sorry about your wife."

"Thanks for bringing Kate over. I was beside myself; I didn't know what to do."

"You did exactly right," Kate said. "There's no other place I want to be than here. Now, when's the last time you got information?"

"Awhile ago. The nurses rush around, but no one tells me anything."

"I'm going to see what I can find out," Kate said. "I'll be right back."

"Okay, sure."

"Why don't we sit down," he suggested, motioning Lance to a nearby chair.

The older man moved slowly and was a bit shaky on his feet but managed to sit down without falling.

"Sorry I ruined your evening," he said.

"You didn't ruin anything. I hope your wife will be all right."

"Bess is a fighter." Lance paused, then looked at him with pain in his blue eyes. "She has always been stronger than me, but she looked...bad. I didn't want to say that to Katie, but I'm scared."

He was scared now, too. Kate's love for her grandparents was huge. He didn't want her to have to deal with losing one.

"Katie is a lot like Bess," Lance continued. "She's forthright, confident, and with the biggest heart. She always goes above and beyond. She's one special girl."

He nodded. "I've seen her go above and beyond."

"But Kate and Bess also carry a lot of pain, a deep wound that has scarred over but has never gone away. That pain comes from my daughter Evie. I don't know if Katie has told you anything about her mother."

"Not a lot," he murmured, but he didn't think Lance was really listening to him. He seemed to be lost in his thoughts.

"Evie is not a bad person, but she's selfish, and she doesn't realize how much hurt she leaves in her wake. She acts impulsively and she's never the one to suffer the consequences. But Katie has paid a price and so has Bess. I shouldn't be thinking about her now, but I can't help wondering if I should call her. If Bess...if she doesn't...well, Evie is her daughter. Does she have a right to know, to be here?" Lance asked.

He had no idea how to answer that question.

Fortunately, Lance didn't seem to really want an

answer—at least not from him.

"But even if I called Evie, would she come?" Lance muttered. "We haven't talked to her in a year. I'm not sure her number is good anymore. But at the end of the day, she's my daughter, Bess's daughter. Shouldn't she know that her mother is in surgery?" He paused, his gaze sharpening. "I'm sorry. I'm rambling on."

"Don't be sorry. Families can be complicated."

"That's for sure. Babies start out all sweet and innocent. It's an instant love affair. You never think you'll want to spend a second away from your child, but then kids grow up, and the distance can be more than you ever imagined." He drew in a shaky breath. "It was bad for us, but it was worse for Katie. She felt the sting of rejection from both of her parents. We tried to make it up to her, take care of her, love her as much as we could, but none of that made up for her not having a mother she could count on—not having a father at all. We used to get so angry with Evie. We'd demand she'd do better, but she just couldn't find it in herself to make that happen. And her father was just a worthless son of a bitch. Did Katie tell you her dad took off after she was born?"

"She mentioned that."

"The two of them didn't care their free love, their bliss, left a little girl without parents to watch over her. That's not love," Lance said scornfully. "Love takes work. It's about putting someone else before yourself. That's what Bess always did. She always put me first, and I tried to do the same." He sent Barrett an agonizing look of desperation. "We've been together so long, I don't remember a time when she wasn't there. I wouldn't know what to do without her.

She's everything."

He could feel the older man's pain. He put a comforting hand on Lance's arm. "Hopefully, you won't have to know. And I have a feeling your Bess would want you to stay positive, keep the faith."

Lance gave him a shaky smile. "That she would. I can be strong for her now. I can believe."

"Yes, you can."

They both rose to their feet as Kate returned. "The surgery is still going on," she said. "The nurse said the doctor will speak to us as soon as it's over."

"I guess we just wait," Lance said wearily, taking a seat once more.

"You can go, Barrett," Kate told him. "It could be awhile."

He knew he should go. He and Kate were barely friends, and he didn't need to be a part of this. She probably didn't even want him to be a part of it, but he found himself reluctant to leave.

He wanted to know if Bess would be all right. He wanted to be there to support Kate and Lance, because they were both really, really shaken. And there was a chance, a terrible chance, that things might get worse.

"You know, I think I'll get us some coffee or tea," he said. "What would you like?"

"It's not necessary."

He glanced over at Lance, who had his head in his hands. "I think maybe some herbal tea."

She nodded. "If they have it."

"You got it. What about you?"

"I'll take a tea, too."

"Done."

She gave him a grateful look. "Barrett, you're being really nice. Thank you."

"It's not a big deal."

"It is—actually. My grandmother is so important to me, even more so to my grandfather. Having you here, well, it makes me feel a little less scared—I don't know why. Maybe because you're so calm."

He was touched by her words and a little unnerved by how close they were getting to each other. She didn't want him to leave, and he didn't want to leave—both desires probably neither one of them could have imagined a few days ago.

"I'll be back in a few minutes," he said, deciding those were the only words he needed to say right now.

——✥✥✥✥✥——

Kate sat down next to her grandfather and put her hand in his, giving him what she hoped was a reassuring smile.

His expression was uncertain and fearful, and that terrified her. Ever since she'd been a little girl, her grandpa had been the male hero figure in her life. He'd been the one to bandage her up after a fall, comfort her with an ice cream sundae after some boy broke her heart, and the only one who could make her smile when she'd waited in vain for her mother to come home and keep whatever promise she'd made her.

But it wasn't just her grandfather who had been there for her; it was her grandmother, too. They were her real parents. They were the people she loved most in the world and she couldn't imagine losing one of them. She kind of wished Barrett hadn't gone to the cafeteria. The man who had annoyed her beyond belief only a few days ago now seemed like a raft in a storm. She missed his strength, his confidence.

Although, that seemed crazy, because he certainly wasn't the most optimistic person she'd ever met.

"Did Barrett leave?" her grandfather asked.

"He went to get you some tea."

"That was thoughtful. He seems like a good man. I just about talked his ear off. But he was a good listener."

"He can be," she said.

"Is he your boyfriend?"

"No. He's my landlord. His family company owns my office building, and he moved in downstairs. We barely know each other."

"But you were out to dinner."

"He was making up for something he'd done. We don't need to talk about him."

"It keeps my mind off your grandmother. Tell me about him. What does he do?"

"He's a divorce attorney, which makes our working situation difficult. This evening, he had a screaming couple in his office, and their argument spilled into the hall, and scared off one of my brides. That's why he took me to dinner—to apologize. I told him when he moved in last week that it wasn't going to work to have our opposing businesses in the same building, but apparently his previous office is under construction or something, and he's not planning on leaving any time soon."

"I'm sure you can find a way to get along. You're good at figuring out what people need and making sure they get it."

She thought about his words. He wasn't wrong. But she wasn't sure she wanted to know what Barrett needed, because if it was anything close to what she was thinking she needed…well, that would definitely not be a need she should try to fulfill.

"I think it's better if we keep our distance," she said.

"Then why is he getting us tea?"

She let out a small, helpless sigh. "I don't really know. He doesn't seem to want to leave."

Her grandfather gave her a compassionate smile. "That's because he likes you, too."

"I never said I liked him."

"I know you well, Katie. And you've been watching that door since he left."

"I'm watching for the doctor."

"You're a very bad liar."

She gave up. "Fine. I do like him, but we don't have much in common. He's cynical, especially when it comes to love, and I'm the eternal optimist."

"You don't have to think exactly the same to fall in love. Your grandmother and I are not the same person. She loves a party and thinks highly of just about everyone she meets. I'd rather sit in my recliner and watch a basketball game, and there are a lot of people I don't care for. Like that guy you used to date, Jimmy something. He always honked the horn for you, and you went running."

"I was seventeen and I thought he was cool."

"He wasn't."

"No, he wasn't," she admitted. "I'd like to think I've gotten a little better at picking out potential boyfriends."

"Or maybe you've just gotten gun-shy. When's the last time you introduced anyone to us? I'm thinking it's been a few years."

"I've been busy building my business, Grandpa."

"You know what they say about all work and no

play..."

"I know that I love my work, and it's where I want to put my time right now. I don't want to give that up for a guy."

"I respect your work ethic and your passion for your job. But it won't keep you warm at night." He took a breath. "You know why Bess and I have lasted as long as we have?"

"Because you really love each other?"

"And because we've always given each other space to grow. You don't have to give up your life to include a man—at least not the right man. He'll be your biggest cheerleader."

She smiled. "Well, I don't see Barrett cheerleading my wedding business. He thinks big weddings set the wrong expectation for a happy marriage."

Her grandfather smiled at her. "I have a feeling you can change his mind."

She wanted to tell him to let it go but talking about her love life seemed to be keeping his mind off her grandmother's surgery, and that was a good thing.

She looked up as Barrett reentered the waiting room and tried to contain the little zing of excitement that ran through her at his presence.

"I have chamomile tea, green tea with honey, and a coffee," he said. "What's your pleasure?"

"I'll have the chamomile," her grandfather said. "It's what Bess likes to drink when she's upset."

"And I'll take the green tea," she said. "Unless you want it?"

"I'm good with coffee," he replied, as he handed out their drinks.

She took a sip of her tea, happy at the rush of

warmth that ran through her. Like her grandfather, she remembered all the times her grandmother had made her a cup of tea and told her to breathe deep and think positively. She definitely needed to do that now.

Barrett sat down next to her and for a few quiet moments, they sipped their drinks and watched the double doors leading into the surgical area. Finally, a doctor in scrubs came through those doors and headed toward them.

They all stood up as the doctor addressed her grandfather.

"We've stopped the bleeding," he said. "She's stable."

"Oh, thank God," she whispered, squeezing her grandfather's hand. "She'll recover completely?"

"We'll be able to tell you more tomorrow, but at the moment it's looking good," the doctor replied.

She could feel her grandfather starting to shake. Before she could move, Barrett came around and put a steadying arm around her grandfather's shoulders.

"Are you all right?" the doctor asked.

"I'm just relieved," her grandfather said, allowing Barrett to guide him back into his chair. "I was so scared."

She gave him a reassuring smile. "Grandma has come this far. She'll make it all the way." She looked back at the doctor. "When can we see her?"

"She'll be sleeping for several hours. I'd suggest you go home and come back in the morning."

"No. I need to be here when she wakes up," her grandfather protested. "She can't be here alone."

"I'll stay," she said immediately. "I'll be with her if she wakes up. You can go home and get some rest and come back in the morning when she's really going to need you, Grandpa. I have to work tomorrow, so tonight will be my shift. What do you say?"

He gave her a doubtful look. "Are you sure?"

"I'm positive."

"I'll drive you home," Barrett offered.

"All right. I can't argue with both of you," her grandfather said. "But, Doc, you sure she's all right?"

"She's doing very well," the doctor said. "I don't expect any changes tonight, but, of course, you'll be notified right away if any issues arise. Now, if you'll excuse me…"

"Thank you," she said, giving the doctor a grateful smile. Then she glanced at Barrett. "My grandfather lives about fifteen minutes away—in the Berkeley Hills. I can give you the address if you want to map it."

"I can tell him how to get there. I haven't lost my mind, Katie," her grandfather said.

"Okay then." She looked at Barrett. "I really appreciate this."

"Why don't you give me your number? I'll check in with you later."

He pulled out his phone and punched in her number, then helped her grandfather to his feet.

"You'll call me if she wakes up at all, right?" her grandfather asked again.

"I promise."

He gave her a kiss on the cheek. "Thank you, Katie."

"You're more than welcome."

She let out a breath as she watched them leave. While Barrett didn't have a hand on her grandfather, he walked right next to him, in case he needed any kind of support. She'd thought she'd hated Barrett.

He'd caused her nothing but problems since he'd moved into the building, but he'd also helped her make favors when her fingers were out of whack and tonight he'd been incredibly supportive. She'd never felt like she'd had anyone but her grandparents who were really in her corner, but tonight she'd had him.

But she couldn't let herself take this all too far...not even in her own head, she told herself. Barrett was a gentleman. He'd been raised to treat people well. She couldn't start thinking it was more than just good manners, could she?

Chapter Ten

"Katie?"

Her grandmother's weak voice brought her eyes open. She'd pulled a chair up next to her grandmother's bed in the middle of the night and had somehow fallen asleep. There was sun coming in the windows now, and her grandmother's blue eyes, so much like her own, were filled with light.

"You're awake," she said, jumping to her feet and smiling down at the woman who meant so much to her.

"Where's Lance?"

"He's at home. He's okay. He'll be back as soon as I call him."

"We were in…an accident."

She nodded, seeing a little confusion in her grandmother's eyes. "Do you remember what happened?"

"No. I hear crashing sounds, and I feel pain in my side." She winced. "Still there but not as bad."

"We'll get you more medication for that. You had surgery last night, but the doctor says you're going to be all right."

"That's good news." Despite her words, her grandmother's gaze turned worried. "Lance had blood on his face. I remember that."

"He just had some cuts. He's fine."

"You're sure?"

"Positive."

"Thank God," her grandmother said with relief.

"Let me call the nurse."

"Call your grandfather first. I want to talk to him. I want to hear his voice."

"Of course." She pulled out her phone and punched in her grandfather's number.

He answered on the second ring. "Katie? Is she awake? Is she all right?"

"Yes, she just woke up. She wants to talk to you." She handed her grandmother the phone.

"Lance, honey, are you all right?" Her grandmother paused, then smiled, as her grandfather's loud, vociferous voice rang through, declaring he was perfect, and she was the one who needed to tell him how she was. And then he finished with a vow of love.

As their conversation turned more intimate, Kate backed out of the room, giving them a little privacy. She told the nurse her grandmother was awake, then used the restroom before making her way back into the room.

"I love you, too," her grandmother said. "And I'm sure Katie won't leave until you get here."

"I won't," she said loudly.

"Did you hear that?" her grandmother asked. "See

you soon." Her grandmother handed her the phone. "He's on his way."

"He was really worried about you last night."

"I'm sorry I gave everyone a scare."

"It's not your fault." She paused, frowning. "Wait a second. How is Grandpa getting here? You only have one car, and he said it was all smashed up."

"I don't know. He said he had a ride. Maybe Hal from next door."

"Oh, of course. Is there anything I can get you?"

"I'm a little thirsty."

She picked up the glass with the straw that had been set next to the bed at some point. She had a feeling she'd missed a lot of what had been going on during the night.

After her grandmother took a few sips, she set the cup back down on the table. "Better?"

"Yes. Your grandpa said you insisted on spending the night here."

"Neither of us wanted you to be alone when you woke up. Grandpa wasn't sure how much you would remember."

"It is fuzzy," she said. "But I know it wasn't your grandfather's fault."

"That's what I understand."

"He said your boyfriend drove him home last night. Did I hear that right? I didn't know you had a boyfriend."

"Barrett is not my boyfriend, and I told Grandpa that. He just didn't want to hear me."

A gleam of amusement appeared in her grandmother's eyes. "That's what he said you said, but he didn't believe you."

"Well, he should have. Barrett is just a friend—

barely that." She paused as a nurse entered the room, along with a different doctor than the one she'd spoken to the night before. They asked her to step outside for a few moments, so she told her grandmother she'd be back soon.

Once in the hallway, she checked her phone for the time. It was almost seven thirty. She would have liked to go home and catch a nap before the day started, but her meeting with the Hunts had been changed from Friday to today at ten o'clock, and she really didn't want to reschedule.

Thankfully, her grandmother seemed to be fine, and she would be able to leave without worrying something major was going to go wrong while she was at work. But she'd feel better once the doctor finished his exam.

She ran through her emails for a few moments, noting one from Jana, her disgruntled bride from the day before. It seemed like a lifetime since all that had happened. Apparently, Jana had gone straight home, spoken to her mother and decided to fire her.

She let out a sigh that was mixed with both disappointment and relief. While she would hate to lose the deposit, Jana Davis had been a very difficult bride so far, and probably in the long run, this was the best thing that could happen. Jana didn't know what she wanted, and she was going to drive everyone crazy trying to figure it out. It irked her that Jana's decision had been spurred on by Barrett's fighting clients but given how much he'd gone out of his way to make that up to her, she could hardly blame him for it.

In fact, the last thing she was feeling right now for Barrett was anger.

She wasn't mad at him at all, not even with this email reminder.

She was missing him, wishing he was here, wishing she could hear his husky voice, see his quirky smile that could be mocking but could also be warm and genuine, and those green eyes of his—so mysterious, so sexy, so penetrating. Just thinking about him sent a shiver down her spine.

She needed to get a grip. Barrett had been a good friend last night. Even before that, he'd been a good dinner companion. She'd been surprised at how easy it was to talk to him, how much more they had in common than she'd first thought.

And he'd opened up to her. He'd told her about Vanessa, about his family, and she doubted that had been easy for him. She didn't think he was a man who liked to fail, and in his eyes, his marriage had been a huge failure. It was why he was so adamant about not ever doing that again. She wanted to believe his opinions would change with time and the right woman, but was that just a foolish daydream? At the end of the day, they were still on opposing ends when it came to love, weddings, and marriage, and she couldn't see that changing any time soon. Getting further involved with Barrett was not a smart idea. She already liked him too much. She needed to get things back on a business-level footing.

As the doctor and nurse exited her grandmother's room, she straightened. "How is she?"

"Doing very well," the doctor replied. "We'd like to keep her another day, possibly two, for recovery and observation, but all her vital signs are good. She should be able to go home by Sunday."

"I'm so relieved."

"She's a strong woman. We'll run more tests later today, but otherwise, I'd expect she'll make a full recovery."

"Thank you."

As the doctor moved down the hall, she saw her grandfather step off the elevator, followed by someone she had not expected to see—Barrett.

He was wearing the same clothes he'd been in the day before, and her stomach twisted with all kinds of mixed emotions.

Her grandfather rushed toward her. "Bess?"

"She's doing well. The doctor just examined her and thinks she can come home by Sunday."

"Thank goodness," he murmured, then pushed his way into the room.

"Barrett," she said, shaking her head in bemusement. "What are you doing here?"

"I gave your grandfather a ride."

"In the clothes you were in last night?"

He shrugged. "I slept at his house. It was late, and he seemed a little shaky. I knew he was going to need a ride this morning, so I figured I might as well crash there."

"I can't believe you did that," she said. "That was really generous."

"It wasn't a big deal. We had a nice chat. He showed me your old room, your photo albums, a couple videos of you dancing the ballet."

She groaned. "He did not do that."

Barrett grinned. "Sorry, but he did. You looked cute in a tutu, but I'm not so sure ballet is your thing."

"It's not. I was terrible. I just liked wearing the outfit." She shook her head again. "I really can't believe he brought those out and made you watch them."

"He needed a distraction. He was kind of wired when we first got there. He wanted to talk."

"What else did you talk about?" she asked a little warily.

"Family stuff." His gaze met hers. "I heard a lot about your mother, a little about your father."

"I'm sure that must have been boring."

"Actually, it was pretty interesting. You told me a little at dinner, but your grandfather filled in the rest of the blanks. I'm beginning to understand why you're so into beautiful weddings and happily ever after. You want what you wished your parents had had."

"That's not the only reason I became a wedding planner. I like events and making people happy and weddings are the biggest, happiest events—at least most of the time."

He gave a nod, but he didn't look like he really believed her. "Well, I'm glad to hear your grandmother is all right. Are you heading back to the city? Or are you going to hang out here?"

"I need to get back. I want to take a quick shower before I go into the office. I have a meeting with Candice and Olivia at ten."

"Why don't I drive you?"

"You're becoming quite the chauffeur," she said lightly. "I'd like to say no, because you've done way too much already, but if you're going into the city, I will take a ride."

"That's where I'm going. I also have a meeting at ten, so…"

"I'll just say good-bye." She opened the door, pausing as her grandfather placed a tender kiss on her grandmother's forehead. Then she said, "Sorry to interrupt, but I need to go to work, if you two will be all right here on your own?"

"Of course," her grandmother said. "But first please introduce me to that handsome man behind you, the one who has taken such good care of Lance."

She glanced back at Barrett, who was hovering in the doorway. "My grandmother wants to say hello."

"I'd love to meet her," he said, following her into the room.

"This is Barrett Fox," she said.

"Pleased to meet you. I'm Bess."

Barrett nodded. "I've heard a lot about you, Bess, from your very devoted husband."

Bess glanced at Lance, then back at Barrett. "I've been blessed. Day I met him was the luckiest day of my life."

"Luckiest day of *my* life," Lance corrected. "We were at a carnival, and she was tossing dimes, trying to win a bowl shaped like a fish, and she wasn't very good at it. So, I stepped up and won it for her."

"I wasn't actually trying to hit the bowl that looked like a fish," Bess put in, a twinkle in her eyes. "I wanted this pretty little candy dish, but when Lance won me the other bowl, I couldn't tell him. We've had that bowl in our cupboard for the last fifty-five years."

"And I didn't know she hated the thing until about two years ago," Lance said. "I overheard her telling the cleaning lady not to break the bowl, because it would break my heart, even if it was ugly as sin."

"Really, Grandma?" she interjected. "You never told him that dish was ugly?"

"I didn't want to hurt his feelings. I felt bad when Lance overheard, but then he told me he'd never liked it, either. We'd both been keeping that a secret. We had a good laugh about it."

"But that's the only lie we ever told each other," her grandfather said, giving his wife a look of love. "We were always honest about everything else."

"Always," Bess agreed. She turned toward Kate. "Now, tell us—how did you and Barrett meet?"

She couldn't help but smile. "He knocked over one of the cupid statues I was storing in his office space and got shot by Cupid's arrow. He was covered in plaster dust, and he was not amused."

Barrett gave her a faint smile. "It's a little funnier now when I think about it. I didn't expect to run into a statue the same height as me."

"I told you they were only supposed to be six inches." She looked at her grandmother. "Barrett was furious. He ordered me to move those statues by Monday. I had to work all weekend to find a place to stash them. We did not start out on a good note."

"But you are friends now," Bess said. "After all he did for your grandfather, how could you not be?"

"We are friends. It turns out he's a much better man than I thought," she said, glancing back at Barrett.

"And Kate is nowhere near as crazy as I first thought," he said, his gaze holding hers for a long few seconds.

"Anyway, we need to go," she said abruptly, letting out a bit of a shaky breath. "We both have work. Do either of you need anything else?"

"We're good," her grandmother said, a twinkle in her eyes. "Thank you, Katie. For staying with me all night."

"You're welcome."

"And thank you, Barrett, for staying with me,"

her grandfather said.

"No problem. I enjoyed getting to know you and watching Kate's ballet recital," Barrett said.

"Oh, you didn't show him those," Bess put in.

Her grandfather gave them a sheepish look. "I thought he'd enjoy it."

"And I did," Barrett said.

"All right, we're going," Kate said decisively. She needed to get Barrett away from her grandparents before they told him more embarrassing stories about her.

They walked out of the hospital and into bright sunshine and crisp, cool air. It was a welcome relief after the stifling medicinal smells of the hospital.

"I feel like I've been here a long time," she said, as she got into Barrett's car.

"Was it a rough night?"

"Not too bad. I think I slept a little in the chair by her bed."

"You are a good granddaughter."

"I wanted to be there for her. And I knew my grandfather needed to rest." She fastened her seat belt as Barrett drove out of the parking garage. "A lot has certainly happened since I interrupted that fight outside your office last night."

He gave her a faint smile. "You can say that again."

"Did you sleep at all?"

"I did—in your old bed," he said. "Although, it was hard to fall asleep looking at posters of boy bands- - and unicorns—an interesting combination of likes, by the way."

"I haven't lived in that bedroom since I was seventeen. At the time, I was boy crazy, and I liked to believe in impossible things—like unicorns. I need to clean that room out, but my grandparents are always resistant when I suggest it, saying I should take time and not hurry through it, that I might want some of my things later even if they don't feel important now. They don't care for change."

"I noticed. But I have to admit, your grandfather's vinyl record collection—that is amazing."

"He's been collecting since he was seventeen. Did he play some records for you?"

"Oh, yeah, a lot of Elvis, a little of the Beatles, and even some Rolling Stones."

"Grandpa used to play guitar in a band when he was young. He has always been into music."

"We played a little together," Barrett said, surprising her with his words.

"You played guitar together?" she asked in astonishment.

"He had two."

"And you play?"

"I'm not bad."

She had a suspicion that was a vast understatement. "I'll bet you're pretty good."

"I can make my way through a song."

"Did you learn when you were young?"

"No. I wanted to, but my mother made me learn the piano. I think that was mostly because she wanted to date the saxophone teacher. That was when she was single, in between the divorce with my father and marrying her second husband. But she lost interest in my musical career once she found out the teacher was dating someone else's mom. I picked up the guitar on my own in middle school. I pretty much taught myself."

"Does your brother play?"

"A little. But not much. Matt tends to be impatient. If he doesn't master something right away, he's over it."

"But you'll take more time to get it right."

"If it's worth doing," he said, shooting her a smile. "Do you play anything?"

"No. I am not musical at all. I can't carry a tune when I sing and trying to read music feels like too much math. My grandfather did try to teach me to play guitar, but it never worked, and we always ended up irritated with each other. Eventually, he gave up on wanting me to play."

"I saw a photo of your mom and your grandfather playing together. She looked like she was a teenager."

"That was at the state fair in Sacramento. She was a singer, songwriter. She tried to make it in music for a while, but then she met my dad and got pregnant and having me derailed her career, at least for a few years. When I was six, she got an offer to sing backup with a country band, and she took it. She left me with my grandparents, and that was the start of her coming and going—mostly going."

"That's not good."

"She was this beautiful creature who would drop into my life every now and then. Once she wasn't tasked with my day-to-day care, she was a lot happier, a lot more fun to be around, but, of course, I couldn't really count on her. Her promises were not worth much. It took me a long time to realize that, to stop being disappointed every time she didn't show up. Eventually, I came to understand she was a free spirit. Or maybe she was just as afraid of commitment as my father was." She blew out a breath, realizing how long she'd been talking. "And, wow, you must be ready to kick me out of this car for talking endlessly about my messed-up family."

"I think I'll make it over the bridge," he said dryly. "And I have first-hand experience with messed-up families."

"Then let's talk about you for a while. What are your parents like?"

"My mother is very tightly wound. She likes everything to be perfect. She plans out her life to the last detail, and she isn't happy when others interfere with her plans. She has a caring heart, but it's not that easy to see. She can be cold and distant until you really get to know her—actually, until she decides she'd like to know you. She's into tennis, golf, and bridge, and enjoys her country-club friends. She's always concerned about what her peers think of her. She's perpetually having cosmetic work done, trying the latest diet, and working out with her personal trainer."

"She must look amazing."

"She's attractive." He paused, shooting her a quick look. "I love her, because she's my mother, but she doesn't always make it easy. She has a lot of opinions, most of which I don't agree with."

"That can be difficult. What's your father like?"

"He's outgoing, loud, loves to tell bad jokes, and thinks he's hilarious. He's charming enough to have found four women who wanted to marry him, and there was never a shortage of women in between those marriages."

"How old were you when your parents split up?"

"I was in the fifth grade."

"That must have been hard on you."

"Frankly, they were fighting so much, I was happy enough when they finally ended it. My mother is much happier with her second husband, and my dad—well, who knows how long this latest marriage will last? His brides get younger and younger, and he is only getting older and older. I don't know why he bothers to keep walking down the aisle. I can't imagine how complicated his alimony payments must be."

"Does he have other children?"

"He has a daughter with his third wife. She's about twelve now. Her name is Daphne, and, no, I haven't spent much time with her. She and her mom moved to Florida after my dad divorced her mother. I believe my father got a vasectomy after Daphne was born, although, I've heard from Matt that his latest wife really wants a child and he's thinking about getting it reversed. That seems crazy, considering he's sixty-seven years old now, but who knows? I've never been able to predict what my father will do."

"Do your parents live in the city?"

"My mother lives in Sausalito—around the corner from the Hunts, in fact. My father lives in a luxury condo downtown. I see my mother about once a month, when she tries to set me up with someone— my dad, every couple of months, usually for a drink or a steak dinner."

His family sounded like they lived a very comfortable, luxurious life, but it didn't seem warm or loving. No wonder Barrett didn't envision a happily ever after for himself.

"Why on earth did you ever pick Vanessa?" she asked. "It sounds like she was a younger version of your mother—a woman you didn't get along with."

"That's a good question. When I first started in law, working at her father's firm, I got caught up in that life, in the social circle we both moved in. We were thrown together at every turn, and there was a lot of pressure from the partners for the young lawyers to have significant others at events. Vanessa fit right in. It wasn't until we started planning the wedding that I began to see the real differences between us. And that year was also a year of changes for me career-wise. I was beginning to realize I didn't want to kill myself working for a big corporate law firm, but I didn't see how I could get out of it. I felt like I was on a runaway train."

"I can see getting swept up in everything. Wedding planning can take on a life of its own," she said.

"That's a generous comment," he said, glancing at her.

"It's true. I've seen a lot of couples lose sight of their priorities. I do try to keep them on track."

"I believe you." He paused as he changed lanes and took the first exit off the bridge. "I thought once we were married and we were back to normal life, things would feel right again, but they never did. We couldn't get along at all. Every day was a new battle. We would look right at each other, but we couldn't really see each other. I wanted out of my career. I wanted out of my marriage. It was a bad situation, and it had to end. My parents and her parents thought we should have tried harder and for a longer time. But we were both done."

"It didn't sound like Vanessa was done the other night. She wanted you to come to her father's party. And she's not engaged anymore."

"Maybe she just had a moment of fond regret. I've seen that with my divorce clients. But it doesn't last. It's really just a wish that things could have been the way you wanted them to be. But they weren't then, and they wouldn't be now."

"I can see that. Even with mothers of the brides, I hear a lot of stories about their love affairs and their weddings. They often want their daughters to recreate their day. They want to be reminded of the moment they said *I Do*, the feelings they had, the hope in their hearts. Not that they're all unhappy now, but I think they just want the reminder. And who am I to judge? I've never made that walk down the aisle, except as a bridesmaid. That I've done five times already."

He smiled as he pulled up in front of her building. "Fortunately, I have not been put in the position of having to do that since my own wedding."

"One day you'll have to stand up for your brother."

"That might be the next time I'm at a wedding."

She smiled back at him. "Well, thanks again for the ride and for everything you've done for me in the last twenty-four hours. If there's anything I can do to repay you, just name it."

"I'll keep that in mind. I think I might like having you in my debt."

She pointed a finger at him. "Don't get any crazy ideas. The swan picture stays."

"Now that I've met your grandparents, I'm a little more appreciative of what the swans mean to you."

"Good." She opened the car door. "I'll see you around."

"I'm sure you will."

Chapter Eleven

—➤➤◄◄◄—

For the next two days, Kate was kept busy with clients, venue tours, and cake tastings. Her meeting with Candice and her mother Olivia Hunt went well, but there were a lot of questions—pointed, probing, and somewhat aggressive questions, some of which she still needed to answer.

Olivia seemed determined to catch her off guard in some way. She also pushed for things that clearly Candice was not interested in having at her wedding. But while Candice spoke up, she usually acquiesced in the end to her more dominant mother.

Kate still had no idea if they were going to retain her services or not. She needed to present a complete proposal by Monday, and then the Hunts would make their decision.

She had a small backyard wedding tomorrow, which fortunately had not required a rehearsal and dinner celebration, so she had a little time tonight to work on her proposal.

Shari came into her office just before five on Friday, a rather odd look in her eyes as she perched on the chair across from her desk. "Are you ready for tomorrow's wedding?"

"It's all set. Vivian and Charles are easy."

"Well, it is the second time for both of them."

"And they're so happy they found each other, they're not too worked up about the wedding."

"That's good," Shari said in a distracted way.

"What's up?" she asked.

"There's something I need to talk to you about, Kate."

She stiffened at Shari's tone. "You sound serious. Please don't tell me you're quitting. If you need a raise, if you need time off—"

"I'm not quitting," Shari said quickly.

"Good. Because I really don't think I could do without you."

"That's nice to hear. What I need to talk to you about doesn't involve work; it's personal. It's about me and Todd."

"What about you and Todd?"

"We haven't been getting along for a while. Our trip to Tahoe was a desperate effort to try to find time to communicate and figure things out, but it didn't really work. I'm meeting with a divorce attorney tonight."

Her heart sank. "Oh, Shari, I'm really sorry to hear this. Are you sure you want to go for a divorce? What about counseling?"

"Todd won't go. I've been begging him for weeks. He said he doesn't need to pay a shrink to tell him what he already knows, that he's not happy. The truth is, Todd is really depressed, and I think it's about more than our marriage, but he won't talk to me, so I can't help. I don't know what to do anymore. I feel like I'm out of options." She drew in a nervous breath. "And there's a bit more."

"What?" she asked warily.

"My appointment is with Barrett. I know you two are at odds, but since he helped with your grandparents the other night, I'm thinking you're not so down on him?"

"I'm not down on him," she said. "I just feel like you're rushing a little, Shari. You haven't even mentioned anything before today."

"I was going to talk to you the day that Barrett moved in downstairs, but you were all worked up about him telling you that your weddings contribute to divorces, and you were so proud that Todd and I were going well. I didn't know how to bring it up."

She sighed. "I had no idea, and I'm sorry you didn't feel like you could talk to me. You have to do what's right for you, and that does not involve worrying about my record as a wedding planner whose couples don't get divorced."

"For the record, our divorce has nothing to do with our wedding."

"I know. And I'm sure Barrett will be a good representative for you. He actually does seem to care about his clients."

"It's just a first meeting. I didn't want you to walk by and wonder what we were talking about."

"Got it. Is there anything I can do?"

"You're doing it. You're being my friend."

"Always. Friends first. Coworkers second." She paused. "When is your meeting?"

"It's in ten minutes. He said he was going to be

working late tonight, preparing for some court appearance tomorrow, and he could fit me in."

"Well, good luck."

"Are you headed home?"

"Actually, I'm going to grab some food and then come back to finish up the proposal for the Hunts."

"What are our odds of getting that job?"

"Probably less than fifty-fifty, but we'll see what kind of magic I can work. I'm having trouble figuring out what Candice really wants and how I can give her that and appease her mother at the same time."

"If anyone can do it, you can. I'll see you Monday."

She nodded, letting out another sigh as Shari left. She felt really bad that Shari's marriage was on the outs but worse that Shari had been so nervous to talk to her. She'd changed her opinion of Barrett days ago; she probably should have filled Shari in on that. She was actually glad that Shari was talking to Barrett. Having gotten to know him better, she thought he would give Shari good advice, and he clearly wasn't in it just for the money, considering he'd walked away from far more lucrative legal work. He really did want to help people. In that way, they were similar.

She turned her attention to her computer and the proposal she was working on, but twenty minutes later, she realized she needed some fuel for the evening ahead.

Grabbing her bag, she headed downstairs. Barrett's outer office door was open, but his private office door was closed. He might still be talking to Shari, or he could just be working. Over the past two weeks, she had often noticed Barrett's lights on as she left for the day. He clearly worked late a lot, as did she. Something else they had in common.

And she really needed to stop thinking about what they had in common and remember all the things they didn't agree on.

Pushing Barrett out of her mind, she headed out the front door and walked down Union Street to her favorite Chinese restaurant.

As she perused the menu, she couldn't decide what she was in the mood for and wound up ordering a couple of dishes. She told herself she'd save whatever she didn't eat for tomorrow, but there was a part of her that wondered if Barrett might want a dinner break. It was probably a bad idea, but she couldn't seem to shake it.

A half hour later, she entered her building and saw that Barrett's inner office door was now open as well. Pausing, she didn't hear Shari's voice, so she walked into the reception area and called out, "Hello?"

"Kate?" Barrett replied. "Come on in."

She moved into his office, relieved that he was alone. She hadn't wanted Shari to think she was intruding on her private meeting.

Barrett got to his feet, a smile on his face, and she couldn't help but smile back.

It had only been two days, but she'd missed him.

"I was just thinking about you," he said.

Her heart skipped a beat. "Really?"

"I was wondering how your grandmother is doing."

"Oh, she's doing well. She is going to come home Sunday probably. She'd like it to be tomorrow, but the docs want to make sure she doesn't have complications from the surgery."

"That's great news. Lance must be thrilled."

"He hasn't left her side."

"I wouldn't have thought otherwise." Barrett paused. "I smell something good. What's in the bag?"

"Chinese food. I have work to do later, and I was hungry. I think I ordered too much. I was wondering if you might want to share, unless you're on your way out, or you have plans. I know it's Friday night." She forced herself to stop talking.

"Apparently, you and I are on the same Friday night track. I have work to do as well. But I could take a break."

"Great."

"Let's go in the conference room," he suggested.

"There's a conference room?" She realized she hadn't really looked at his office since the first day when he'd still been remodeling.

He led her out of his office and through the reception area to a small conference room. He flipped on the lights and moved over to a fridge. "I have beer, white wine, and soda."

"A beer sounds good," she said, setting the bag of food on the table, as she took off her coat and sat down.

Barrett came back with two beers and a couple of paper plates, then took the seat across from her.

She started opening containers. "I hope you like what I ordered. I have chicken chow mein, sweet and sour pork, egg rolls, rice, and Kung Pao chicken."

He raised an eyebrow. "And you were going to eat all this yourself?"

"Well, not in one sitting, but Chinese food is always good the next day. Help yourself." As he put some pork on his plate, she said, "Shari told me she was meeting with you about a possible divorce. I was really surprised that her marital problems had gotten to that point. I guess I haven't been paying attention."

"I'm sure you saw what she wanted you to see."

"Maybe. Or I wasn't paying enough attention. Shari was afraid to ruin my record of happy brides and lasting marriages. I mentioned that you'd suggested out-of-this-world weddings contributed to divorce."

"That was a generalization," he admitted.

"Of course it was. I know it wasn't the wedding that caused their problems. I'm just sorry she didn't feel like she could tell me."

"She told you now."

"Do you think there's any chance they can work things out?"

"I don't know. That's on them."

"But you'd encourage it, right?"

"I always do. I prefer my clients come to me when they've exhausted all possibility of reconciliation. Then they are much more focused in their thinking. By the way, this is good," he added, as he scooped up another bite of chicken chow mein. "Where's the restaurant?"

"About three blocks down the street. I know all the best take-out places on Union Street, if you're interested."

"I'll keep that in mind."

"Where was your other office?"

"Downtown, near Union Square."

"And a pipe broke?"

"Yes. It flooded the entire floor. Then more problems were discovered, so there's a lot of remodeling going on."

"But you'll go back."

"It was a good location. Better parking than

around here, but I have to admit this old house is growing on me. Aside from the parade of brides and their mothers going up and down the stairs."

"It hasn't been that bad."

He grinned. "No, it hasn't. So, what do you have going on this weekend?"

"I have a backyard wedding tomorrow. It's an older couple—one a widower, the other a divorcee, so it's a second wedding. They're so happy and chill that it's been really easy to plan. It's going to be a short ceremony followed by a beautiful lunch and then they're off to Bali."

"That sounds like a decent plan."

"They definitely wanted something intimate and personal."

"I'm surprised they hired a planner."

"They both have big jobs and children, and they wanted me to take care of all the details: the flowers, the music, the photography, the food, etc. It was actually a nice change, and they have been great to work with."

"Do you ever get to just have fun on a weekend?"

"Sometimes, but I like to be busy on the weekends; that usually means business is good."

"Would you ever hire someone to help? Or does Shari cover the weddings as well?"

"No. Shari doesn't do the weddings. She handles all our financials and our paperwork and the stuff I am not as good at. But dealing with the brides, their families, and the actual wedding is not her thing. I, on the other hand, think that's the most fun."

"Then you're in the right business."

"I know I am. What about you? What are you doing this weekend?"

"Tomorrow, I'm going to run a 5K down the Great Highway and through the zoo in a fundraising race for diabetes research. My grandfather had diabetes, and I grew up watching him give himself shots. He eventually died from the disease. Since then, the Fox Foundation has been a sponsor of this particular race."

"That's great. I didn't realize your family had a foundation."

"Both Matt and I are on the board. My father used to be involved but not so much anymore. Philanthropy is not really his thing. He prefers work that increases his profit margins." He paused. "Too bad you're busy—you could have joined me."

"I could have cheered you on at the finish line, but I'm not in condition to run a 5K. Are you?"

"I've run three times this week, so I'm ready."

"When do you have time to run?"

"When I first wake up."

"But it's so cold in the mornings right now."

He laughed. "Not once you start running. You should come out sometime."

"I might get on a bike but running is not my thing."

"Then maybe we'll do a bike ride one day."

She liked the sound of that, only because it involved them getting together again. No matter how many times she told herself to just say goodbye to him and mean it, she couldn't seem to actually do it.

"Are you working on last-minute wedding prep tonight?" he asked.

"No, tomorrow is set. I'm trying to finalize my proposal for the Hunts. They want to see three scenarios with different venues and different price points. They want me to surprise them with my amazing creativity," she added. "That's a direct quote from Mrs. Hunt. In other words, if I don't knock their socks off with some idea that they never would have thought of themselves, I probably won't get the job."

"Do you have any amazing ideas?"

"The problem is that what I think Candice will love, I don't think Olivia will. And I have to please both of them." She let out a sigh. "Right now, it feels fairly impossible. But I have to find a way. It's a huge job."

"What does Candice want? It seems like pleasing her is the priority."

"It is, but I want to make both of them happy."

"I've known the Hunts for a long time, and rarely do Candice and her mother agree on anything."

"That's not helpful."

"Sorry. Tell me some of your ideas. Maybe I can help."

"Olivia wants a hotel venue like the Fairmont, the Four Seasons, that kind of thing, but Candice is more interested in a Napa winery or an art museum."

"They have weddings in museums?"

"Yes, there are spaces that are rented out for weddings at a lot of places in the city that you would never imagine. I have found a couple of intriguing options. One is an artist's collective in the South of Market area. It's in an old warehouse and the space is beautiful and artsy. There's a dance floor, plenty of room for tables, a kitchen for catering, and it has a cool, hip vibe."

"Olivia is going to hate that."

She frowned at his words, but they echoed her own thoughts. "I know. But I think Candice would like it."

"What else do you have?"

"There's a mansion on Nob Hill that can be rented for weddings. It's very elegant, lovely views, but it feels too close to the environment the Hunts actually live in." She paused. "What does Olivia like? What do you know about her that I don't? Does she love books? Because the new library has a room that's available for rental."

"I've never seen her read, but you know what she does like—gardens. A long, long time ago, before she married her husband and had kids, she studied to be a landscape designer. Her only dislike of her Sausalito home is that there isn't enough flat land for a big garden."

At his words, a new idea began to take root in her brain. "The Conservatory of Flowers in Golden Gate Park does weddings. I wonder if that would work."

"Maybe. Are Candice and Anthony going to have a church wedding?"

"Olivia wants that, but Candice told me privately she'd rather not do it in a church. Maybe that's the trick—I convince Olivia to let Candice skip the church wedding and have both the ceremony and the reception at the conservatory. That will work for at least one of the three ideas I need to have. Any other great thoughts? Anything Candice particularly likes?"

He thought for a moment as he finished eating. "She loves the cable cars. Whenever we would go to the city, she always wanted to take a ride."

She considered his words. "Maybe I could build something around a cable car...perhaps a parade of cable cars to the wedding venue. We could rent the ones that don't run on the tracks. That would be a different idea versus just your ordinary limo. You're pretty good at this, Barrett."

He laughed. "I'm just telling you what they like. You're taking it to another dimension."

"Well, I appreciate the tips. I was really stumped, but if I think gardens and cable cars, creative and elegant, maybe I can figure out a way to merge it all in an amazing way."

"I think you're up to the challenge. When does this have to happen?"

"By Monday morning. I just have to keep thinking outside of the box."

"What's your vision of a perfect wedding?"

"You mean for myself?"

"Yes. Surely you've thought about it. How could you not?"

"I do get ideas, but then they change, and I think of something else. I go back and forth on what I'd want."

"But it will be big, grand, crazy?"

"I don't know about that. I honestly don't have that much family, and while I have my core group of friends, it's not like I'd be inviting a huge crowd. I guess it depends on who I marry and what they want. But no matter how big or how small, I just want it to feel romantic, tender, loving, joyful, intimate." She cut herself off, realizing she was getting carried away. "Anyway…that's probably enough wedding talk for you. I'm surprised you lasted this long."

"You did feed me; it was the least I could do. Sorry, we didn't leave you anything for leftovers."

"It's fine. I'm glad you enjoyed it." As their gazes met, she drew in a quick breath. "I should go upstairs and start working."

"I should go to my office and start working." Despite his words, Barrett made no effort to get up. Instead he said, "It was nice of you to share your dinner with me."

"It was the least I could do. I still owe you for spending the night with my grandfather and watching movies of me trying to do ballet."

"You're gifted in a lot of areas, but I'm not sure dance is one of them."

"Believe me, I know."

"The ballet world's loss is the wedding world's gain."

She laughed. "Well said. But seriously, Barrett, I do feel I owe you for what you did for my grandparents."

"You don't owe me anything. And you just bought me dinner."

"It's not enough. What else can I do?"

He thought for a moment. "Well, if you really want to repay me…" He paused, then shook his head. "No, it's probably a bad idea."

"What's the idea?"

"It doesn't matter."

"Just tell me."

"My mother is having her sixty-fifth birthday party on Sunday night, and she keeps telling me about all the single daughters of her friends who will be there. If I were to bring a date, I wouldn't have to feign interest in any of them."

"What if one of them is perfect for you?"

"I'm not worried about that. But, like I said, it's probably not a good idea, because my mother is a wild card. She can be charming and gracious. She can be angry and vindictive. She can be your best friend or your worst enemy."

"A real Dr. Jekyll and Mr. Hyde. I'm both scared and intrigued. Would she care if you bring a date?"

"She'd probably love it. She is dying for me to give up my single status and give her some grandchildren. I've told her to put her money on Matt for both of those events, but she doesn't give up easily. When she gets stuck on a thought in her head, she just can't let it go."

"It's normal for parents to worry about their kids. She wants you to be happy."

"I know, and while I normally avoid any party she throws, it is her birthday. There will be plenty of food and drink, and you might make some good contacts. As I mentioned, she has a lot of friends with daughters and sons who might be getting married in the next few years."

"Now you're appealing to my business interests."

"Is it working? You know what—forget I said anything. I didn't hang out with your grandfather to put you in my debt. It was just the right thing to do. He was upset. He was alone. And it wasn't a hardship for me."

"Most people would have just dropped him off and left. I'll be your date Sunday night. I'd like to meet your mother and your brother."

"If you're sure."

"I'm sure. Is it fancy? What should I wear?"

"Some kind of sparkly cocktail dress."

"I can do that." She got to her feet. "I better get to work."

"I can clean this up," he said, as he stood up.

"All right." She hesitated, then impulsively leaned over and gave him a quick kiss.

He stared back at her, his green eyes darkening. "That was nice—but a little fast."

"Because it's good night." As she turned to leave, he grabbed her wrist.

"This is good night," he said, right before he gave her a long, passionate kiss that sent her head spinning.

"That was better," she agreed, her nerves tingling all over.

"Still too short."

"Not considering we both have work to do."

"I suppose."

"I'll see you Sunday." It took all of her willpower to walk out of the conference room. Then she ran up the stairs, before she could change her mind.

Chapter Twelve

—⇒⇒⟨⟨⟨—

Sunday evening seemed to take forever to arrive. While Kate had been busy with the wedding on Saturday and had spent most of the morning working on the Hunts' proposal, she'd still had plenty of time—too much time—to think about Barrett, and she had to admit she was excited to see him again. She didn't know where they were going in their relationship, and she was afraid to question any of it, because she doubted she would like the answer. But for now, she just wanted to have a good time.

When she opened the door and saw his handsome face, a shiver ran down her spine. He looked spectacularly handsome in his charcoal gray suit, his face freshly shaven, his dark hair styled but one errant wave still falling sexily over his forehead. And his eyes—so green, so penetrating, so damned compelling. It was difficult to look away.

Barrett didn't seem to want to look away, either, his gaze traveling down her clingy dark-red cocktail dress that she really hoped was appropriate for his mother's party.

"You're beautiful, Kate," he murmured, an appreciative gleam in his eyes that only made another shiver run down her spine.

"You look good, too." She forced herself to breathe. "Do you want to come in or shall we just go?"

"I'd rather come in and stay in, but…"

"We need to get to your mom's house, because it's her birthday, and you're being a good son."

"Unfortunately, yes."

"Okay." She grabbed her wrap and bag from the side table. "I'm ready." She pulled the door closed behind her and locked it and then followed Barrett out to his car. "I'm a little nervous," she confessed, as she slid into the passenger seat.

He shot her a quick look. "Really? I would think parties are your sweet spot."

"When I'm working a party, I know exactly what I'm doing. But this is different; it's your mom's birthday party, and I'm a little worried that she won't be happy you're bringing a complete stranger."

"Trust me, she'll be thrilled I brought a date.

———◆◆◆———

Barrett could not have been more wrong.

As Kate shook hands with his mother, Pamela Carlton, a tall, attractive brunette, she was given a frosty, annoyed smile. Then Pamela turned to her son with a pointedly irritated look.

"I didn't realize you were bringing a date, Barrett."

"You said I should," he replied.

"And you said you weren't even sure you were coming, much less bringing anyone."

"Things changed. Is there a problem?"

She hesitated, then said, "I suppose it's fine."

Kate was a little shocked at how rude Pamela was being. She could not have made her feel more unwelcome, and she wondered why Barrett's mother had taken such an instant dislike to her. All she'd said was hello.

As Pamela waved them into the house, a woman dressed in black slacks and a black shirt came over to take Kate's wrap and bag. She was followed by a waiter, who handed them two glasses of champagne.

Kate was more than happy to have a little bubbly to get this party started.

"How do you know my son, Miss Marlow?" Pamela asked as they hovered in the entry. It felt like Pamela wasn't sure she wanted them to come all the way into the party.

"Please call me Kate," she said, putting on a polite smile. "Barrett moved his law firm into my building last week. I have the office upstairs."

"Oh, right, the Victorian. Matt said you'd decided not to work in the tower, Barrett, although I can't imagine how this old house space could be better."

"It suits me fine," Barrett said. "And it allowed me to meet Kate. She's a wedding planner. In fact, she's talking to Candice and Olivia about doing Candice's wedding."

"Well, how lovely," Pamela said. "The Hunts will be here tonight. I'm sure they'll be happy to see their possible wedding planner."

Kate inwardly winced at the thinly veiled insult.

Barrett's mother had made her sound like a servant.

"Mom," Barrett said, a warning note in his voice. "Don't make me sorry I came."

"To your mother's birthday? How could you possibly be sorry? I'm just a little on edge, because, well, there's no easy way to say this, but Vanessa and her parents are coming."

"What? Are you serious?" he asked. "Why on earth would you invite Vanessa?"

Kate drew in a breath as the tension between mother and son literally crackled the air. Barrett was furious, and Pamela was defiant.

"We are family friends," Pamela said. "I didn't think you would be bringing anyone. You should have told me."

"Maybe I should go," she murmured softly.

Barrett grabbed her hand and squeezed her fingers, shooting her a look that begged her not to make good on that suggestion. As much as she wanted to turn and flee, she did owe him for the kindness he'd shown her grandfather.

"You're not going anywhere without me," he said firmly. "If my mother wants you to leave, then I'll go with you."

"Don't be ridiculous. No one has to leave," Pamela said quickly. "I was just giving you a heads-up. There are lots of people here; I doubt you'll even have to speak to Vanessa. I just thought...well, it doesn't matter now what I thought." She paused. "I need to check with the caterer. I'll speak to you later."

"Barrett, I should go," she said, as his mother left. "She doesn't want me here."

Before Barrett could respond, his name rang out.

She turned to see another man approaching, one

with brown hair, green eyes, and features very similar to both Barrett and his mother.

"Hello, big brother," the man said, with a charming grin. "You made it."

"Barely. Thinking about leaving."

"Why? You just got here. And you haven't introduced me to your date."

"This is Kate Marlow, the wedding planner from my office building—my brother Matt."

She couldn't help noting the fact that Barrett had felt it necessary to qualify her presence, as if he didn't want Matt to get the idea that she was someone he was interested in.

"Nice to meet you, Kate," Matt said, with none of the cool bitterness his mother had expressed.

"You, too." She was relieved to find not everyone in Barrett's family was going to hate her on sight.

"I'm glad you came. I'm sure Mom is thrilled you brought someone," Matt added.

"I wouldn't call her reaction thrilled," Barrett said tightly. "She apparently invited Vanessa and her parents, and now she's realizing it might be awkward."

"Because I'm here," Kate put in.

"Ah," Matt said with understanding. "Well, it doesn't have to be awkward. It's a big party. You don't have to talk to Vanessa. And it's not like you broke up yesterday. It's been years."

"I know. I don't care that Vanessa might be here; I care that Mom treated Kate poorly because of it."

"I'm sure she was just taken aback," Kate told him, realizing he still had hold of her hand. "Don't worry about it. I'm fine. I don't offend that easily. You should hear how some mothers of the bride talk to me."

"You're being too generous," he told her.

She smiled at him. "I have champagne. It's all good. Family is family. I don't judge."

"That's good," Matt put in. "Because our family is a little crazy."

"I'm no stranger to family crazy," she said lightly.

"Where's the beautiful Amy?" Barrett asked his brother. "Has she dumped you already?"

"Surprisingly, no." Matt tipped his head to the redhead who was now talking to his mother.

Kate was a little shocked to see Pamela smile with real pleasure at the young woman. *So Pamela wasn't cold as ice with everyone, only with her.*

"That's Amy," Matt said. "She knows my mother from the tennis club. In case you were wondering why they're so friendly."

She nodded. "That makes sense."

"And I can shed a little light on the Vanessa invitation," Matt added. "Since Mom found out Vanessa's engagement is off, she got it in her head that maybe there's a chance Vanessa and Barrett can get back together."

"That's ridiculous," Barrett said.

"I told her she was out of her mind, but she doesn't listen to me," Matt replied. "Anyway, I'm going to join Amy and Mom. I'll talk you up, Kate. I've got your back."

"You really don't have to bother."

"It's no bother." He turned to Barrett. "Why don't you get Kate some food, mingle with our old family friends, try to look like it's a party and not an execution?"

"I'm not sure I can do that," Barrett muttered.

As Matt left, she squeezed Barrett's hand. "I

really am okay, Barrett. And I like your brother."

His tension eased at her words. "Matt is very likeable. Much more than me."

"One thing I don't understand…"

"What's that?"

"You said your mother set you up with the woman you took to the Winter Ball. Why would she do that if she wants you back with Vanessa?"

"She must not have known at the time that Vanessa was no longer engaged." He paused, giving her an apologetic look. "I never imagined she would treat you like that, Kate. She can be cold, but she's usually polite."

"What's her husband like?"

"James is a great guy. He's a little too talkative about really boring topics, but he treats my mom well, and they seem to be happy together. That's him—the balding man by the window."

She nodded, then turned as a rush of cold air hit her. Coming through the front door was Vanessa, followed by a silver-haired gentleman and a very thin, older brunette, who was probably Vanessa's mother. "Look who's here," she muttered.

"Barrett, it's good to see you," Vanessa's father said, striding forward.

Barrett let go of her hand to shake hands with his former father-in-law. "Doug, Mary," he added, nodding to Vanessa's mother. "Vanessa." He then reached for her hand once more. "This is Kate Marlow."

As he made the introductions, she smiled at everyone, noting a hint of pain in Vanessa's gaze.

"How's business, Barrett?" Doug asked.

"It's very good."

"No shortage of couples breaking up, huh?" Doug continued.

"Not so far, no."

"And what do you do, Miss Marlow?" Vanessa asked.

"I'm a wedding planner."

Vanessa raised one of her finely penciled eyebrows. "You plan weddings and Barrett negotiates divorces? That's odd."

She shrugged. "It has been interesting sharing office space. Our clientele is at opposite ends of the happiness spectrum."

"And your opinions about marriage and weddings must also be in opposition," Vanessa said, her gaze flitting from Barrett to her. "Barrett blamed our wedding for everything that went wrong in our marriage. Did he tell you that?"

"He mentioned it. I know he's not a fan of weddings," she murmured.

"He doesn't ever want to get married again," Vanessa continued. "Isn't that true, Barrett? Isn't that what you told me?"

Barrett drew in a breath. "I don't think we need to get into old history."

"Vanessa, Doug, Mary," Pamela exclaimed, coming over to greet her friends.

Kate was actually relieved by his mother's interruption.

Barrett took advantage of her appearance to pull her away from the group. "Let's get out of here."

"Really? Are you sure? Your mom will be disappointed if you leave." As much as she was happy to go, she didn't want to become a wedge between Barrett and his mother.

"I'm positive. I'm not going to put up with anyone disrespecting you, not even if it's my mother."

She was more than a little touched by his words, although she couldn't help pointing something out. "You don't really respect what I do, either."

"I respect you." He looked deep into her eyes. "And I like you, Kate."

"I like you, too," she murmured, feeling the unmistakable heat running between them.

"Then let's get out of here." He started to turn, then paused. "Unless you want to wait for the Hunts to arrive, so you can schmooze with them?"

"No. I turned in my proposal this morning, so whatever they decide is up to them."

"Then let's get out of here."

They grabbed her bag and wrap out of a guest room and slipped out of the house.

"So, what's your favorite place to eat?" he asked, as they walked to the car.

She thought for a moment. "There's a place near the Sausalito Harbor that serves tapas and really good wine."

"You're on," he said, flashing her a smile. "That sounds a lot better than this."

She thought so, too.

Barrett had made the right decision. Getting Kate out of his mother's house had been a far better idea than ever getting her into it.

At a table by the café window overlooking the harbor lights, they shared small plates of honey-rubbed ribs, roasted carrots, patatas bravas, sesame seed crusted salmon and a kale salad with cranberries, coconut and pumpkin seeds. In the warm, cozy restaurant with good food and good wine, he felt infinitely more relaxed.

The conversation flowed easily, and Kate's blue eyes sparkled as she regaled him with crazy wedding stories.

"I know I'm just making you hate my business even more," she said, as she sipped the last of her wine.

"Actually, I'm just amazed at how many different ways people want to say I Do. The horses on the beach at sunset were clearly fraught with problems from the onset."

"I know, and I tried to talk them out of it. I said there might be fog or the horses could spook, or, you know, go to the bathroom at an inappropriate time, and they said they were confident it would all go well."

"But it didn't. Everything you just said went wrong."

"I will never do horses again," she said with a laugh. "I'm not big on boat weddings, either. Someone always gets seasick, sometimes me."

He smiled at her self-deprecating humor. He liked how real Kate was. There was absolutely no pretense about her. She was who she was, and she was proud of it. She genuinely liked herself, and that was rare in most people he knew.

"Can I just say again how sorry I am that I introduced you to my mother?" he asked.

"I'm sure we just caught her off guard. When she saw me, she realized that there was going to be awkwardness with Vanessa, and she didn't know what to do about it."

"That's no excuse. I'm going to talk to her about it tomorrow."

"You don't need to do that, Barrett."

"I do need to do that," he reiterated. "My mother needs to understand that she has nothing to say about my life, and she needs to treat anyone I bring over to her house with respect. Otherwise, I won't be coming over."

"I just don't want to come between you."

"Trust me, this conversation is long overdue."

"I'm sure she wants the best for you."

"What she thinks is the best. She's always been controlling, but I have to admit she shocked me tonight. She's never been that overtly obnoxious. It was embarrassing."

"Well, you can't pick your family. God knows my mother is no prize. She's not snobby, but she's flaky and unreliable. She likes to chase whatever shiny new penny catches her eye. And she doesn't think much about the consequences of any of her actions. She's a very selfish person, although she would never describe herself that way. She thinks she's amazing and other people just don't understand her creative mind."

"Other people like your grandparents?" he asked.

"They are definitely at the top of the list. The three of them don't get along, and my mother has never expressed any thanks to her parents for raising me."

"Lance mentioned he wasn't sure if he should call your mother when Bess got hurt. He was rattled about it. But in the end, I think he decided not to."

"Which was the best decision. Although, she

might not have come even if she knew."

He heard the bitter pain in her voice and had a feeling Kate had been hurt a lot by her mother. He hated that his mother had done the same thing to her. She didn't deserve to be hurt by anyone, much less two women who weren't even in her league.

"Did your grandmother come home today?" he asked, wanting to ease the tension on Kate's face.

She nodded. "Yes. She's doing really well. She really does bounce back fast from any adversity."

"That's great."

"I'm very relieved. It could have been so much worse. I'm trying to convince them not to get a new car, since their old one is out of commission, but I'm not sure I'll succeed. I know they don't drive the freeways anymore, and this accident wasn't their fault, but I still worry."

"It's hard to give up the freedom that driving brings," he said.

"I know, which is why I haven't pushed. They're both in good mental shape. I just don't know how good their reflexes are. Anyway, I'll go see them sometime this week and talk about it with them." She set her empty wineglass down. "What do you have going on the next few days?"

"I have a mediation that will probably take most of tomorrow and then some meetings later in the week. What about you?"

"I have a busy schedule, too. A lot of brides start shopping now for summer and fall weddings. I have a couple of bands to listen to, some venues to visit, florists to talk to, wedding dress designers to interview, and of course cakes to taste—my favorite part of the job."

He was amazed at all the different details she had to deal with. "You must have built a good network of vendors by now."

"I have, and most of the time I use them, but sometimes brides want something different or someone of their own choosing. I'm sure if I get Candice's wedding, I'll be using her mother's vendors. And that's fine. I can work with anyone." She paused. "But what I'm most excited about this week is Friday night's bridal shower for Jessica and Maggie. It's a couples' shower, so more of a party than a traditional shower. It has been awhile since we've all gotten together."

There was affection in her voice and a wistfulness in her gaze. He suspected Kate was a very loyal person. Once you were her friend, you were a friend for life. "That sounds like fun. I didn't know there were couple showers."

"It's all the rage. Just like the couple favors."

"Right. I forgot about those. Do you have weddings next weekend, too?"

"No, but I am working a bridal fair on Saturday."

He shook his head in bemusement. "You weren't kidding when you said your schedule was packed. And I have to say it sounds like more fun than mine."

"It is fun, not that brides can't be picky and annoying."

"All clients can be picky and annoying," he returned. "Where's the bridal shower at?"

"Andrea and Alex's house, which is a mansion with a huge game room that the guys will enjoy, I'm sure."

"What kind of games?"

"All the games that Alex's company makes, like

Raven, *Fire Flight,* and *Vertigo*. He basically has an arcade at his house."

"I've been playing *Vertigo* since version one. I can't believe you know the guy who invented it."

"I'm surprised you like video games. I thought you liked to run and bike."

"I do, but Matt and I also played a lot of video games when we were kids," he confessed. "I must admit I still occasionally play when I'm killing time on a Sunday."

She smiled. "As a guilty pleasure, it's not that bad. Whenever we get together at Alex's house, all the guys end up in the arcade at some point."

"What's Donovan like? Is he a kid at heart?"

"Definitely. He's a great guy, very down-to-earth. You wouldn't know he's rich. He also does a lot for underprivileged children, so there are often kids around. You'd like him." She paused, giving him a thoughtful look. "You know, you could come with me."

"To your friends' bridal shower? I doubt they'd like that."

"They'd like it more than your mother did when I showed up at her birthday party," she said dryly.

"That was bad," he admitted. "I'd like to avoid a repeat."

"There wouldn't be a repeat. They would welcome you. You should come, Barrett. Actually, you'd be doing me a favor. As the last single girl standing in the group, it would be nice not to go alone. Unless, of course, you're busy."

He should say no. Bridal showers weren't his thing, especially for people he'd never met. On the other hand, he liked spending time with Kate, and meeting the maker of *Vertigo* would be interesting. "If you're sure no one will care…"

"It will be fine. Like I said, I'm the organizer. While Andrea is hosting, I'm handling the food and drinks and there will be plenty."

"Then it's a date."

She licked her lips. "We've made a lot of dates considering we're not dating."

"I was thinking that, too," he said with a smile. "But as long as we're having fun…"

"Right. It's just fun. It doesn't mean anything."

At her words, he wondered if she wanted it to mean something.

Frowning, he wondered if he wanted it to mean something, too.

Chapter Thirteen

It was a little too quiet in the car, Kate thought, as Barrett drove her home.

After dinner, they'd taken a walk around the harbor, looking at Sausalito's famous floating homes, that were as rebellious and vibrant as ever. While they'd both agreed they liked the idea of living a free-spirited life on a boat in the harbor, it would probably stress them both out to be in such a small space. And while rocking back and forth might be soothing for a while, it didn't seem like a long-term proposition. They both had too much energy, too much drive.

They'd also done a little window-shopping. Barrett found her fascination with boots quite amusing, and she'd been surprised at how much time he'd spent looking at houses for sale on the window of a real-estate office. For a man who seemed to have no interest in commitment, he seemed incredibly interested in owning a home one day.

Barrett had given her his coat as they strolled,

since she hadn't really dressed for being outside, and with his hand in hers, she felt warm and toasty despite the cold, clear night.

She still had the coat on now, even though Barrett had fired up the heater once they'd gotten in the car. But she wasn't ready to give it up just yet.

In some ways, the coat felt like a metaphor for their relationship—something that she wanted to hold on to, but she knew she couldn't. *It was just for now, not forever.*

She didn't know what Barrett was thinking about, but while the conversation had been easy and fun all evening, once they had gotten into the car, it seemed to evaporate.

She was starting to feel tense, expectant, and unsure. The night had started out as a favor to Barrett, but it had turned into more than that. Since leaving his mom's house, she'd seen yet another side of Barrett, one that felt younger, more relaxed, more fun.

She could hardly correlate this man with the one who'd been so angry and uptight the first night they'd met. "What changed?" she asked, not realizing she'd spoken aloud until Barrett glanced in her direction.

"What?" he asked in confusion.

"I was just thinking how different you seem tonight versus the man who knocked over my statues and yelled at me two weeks ago."

"I didn't yell."

"You were really angry. But now that I know you better, I have to say I don't understand why you got so mad. You seem able to take a joke. What changed?"

His jaw tightened as he came to a stop at a traffic light. "I was having a bad week when we first met, and I was not in the mood for romantic cupid statues."

His words made her curious. "What had happened?"

He hesitated, then said, "The day before I ran into you, my father's fourth wife, Tanya, had asked me to meet with her at a house she and my dad were looking to buy. I didn't know why she wanted my opinion; we're not close. But I agreed to check it out. When I arrived, I found out she was less interested in my real-estate advice and more interested in what my father had been doing while he worked late in his office the night before."

"That doesn't sound good."

"It wasn't good. After the water pipe broke in my office, I spent a couple of days in the tower where Fox Management is located. I had been in the office the previous night when my dad told Tanya he had to work late. I had seen him leave five minutes later, and he had not been on his way home."

"Where did he go?"

"I have no idea."

"What did you tell Tanya?"

"I said I didn't keep track of my father, and she should ask him if she had concerns."

"How did she take that?"

"She started crying."

"Oh, damn."

He frowned as he gave a nod. "It was not fun. I finally calmed her down, offered her some probably worthless reassurances and took off."

"Would your father cheat on his wife?"

He sighed. "I don't know. We don't talk about things like that. In my experience, he usually just gets a divorce when he's done with a relationship. After that conversation, I sped up my timetable to get out of the tower. The next day, I looked at our list of unoccupied spaces and decided the old Victorian on Union Street was perfect. It just needed a little remodeling, but that didn't worry me, because we have crews ready to go. Our company manages a lot of buildings." He paused, as he took a moment to concentrate on the narrowing lanes of the Golden Gate Bridge. Once they were through the toll plaza, he said, "Anyway, you know what happened next. I ran into your cupids, and I wasn't in the mood for your romantic joke."

"That Cupid shot his arrow at you?"

"That's the one."

"I was trying to lighten the mood."

"I know, and I had no sense of humor that night. Cupid's arrow might bring love but is it ever worth the trouble? The pain? The problems? The inevitable ending?"

"It's not inevitable. Look at my grandparents."

"Maybe they're the exception to the rule. Look at your parents—at my parents."

"We do come from screwed-up families," she admitted.

"Makes me wonder how we turned out so well," he said lightly.

She met his smile with one of her own. "Good question."

He turned at her street and slowed down, searching for a parking spot.

"You can just drop me off," she said.

"No, I'll walk you up." He pulled over just down the block from her building.

She licked her lips, wondering what would happen at her door.

Should she ask him in? Suggest coffee? But where would that lead? And if it led where she thought, was she ready to go there? They'd been flirting with the line between friends, associates, tenants…should she cross that line, obliterate it altogether?

Barrett didn't say anything as they made their way into her building and up the stairs to her apartment. He waited while she unlocked the door and pushed it open. She stepped inside and turned on the light. He hovered in the doorway.

"Everything good?" he asked, his gaze scanning the room.

She nodded. "Yes."

"I guess I'll go then."

"That's probably best," she said. "We both have a lot of work this week. We'll touch base about the shower in a few days."

"That sounds good. If you change your mind about me coming—"

"I won't," she said, wishing the shower was tomorrow, because that would give her an excuse to see him again. Next Friday seemed like a long time to wait.

"Okay."

He stepped forward, his hands coming to rest on her shoulders. Her heart sped up.

"I'm going to need my coat," he said.

"Oh, yes, of course," she said.

"But first…" He stopped her as she started to take off his coat.

She caught her breath at the purposeful look in his eyes. She felt like she was sixteen again, ridiculously nervous about what would be a simple good night kiss.

But when his mouth covered hers, there was nothing simple about it.

There was heat and desire and a deep-gutted yearning for more. Their lips clung together as he pulled her up against his chest, as the kiss between them belied all the lies they'd told themselves about their barely there friendship.

She threw her arms around his neck, pulling him back for another kiss, until they finally had to take a breath.

Barrett's green eyes were glittering with fire, his breath ragged and hot, and her heart beat even faster. She wanted this man. *But...*

"Kate?" he murmured, a questioning note in his voice.

She tried to draw a breath, but her chest was tight, a dozen thoughts racing around her head, her body at war with her brain.

"We...shouldn't," she managed to get out.

He stared back at her, his gaze unreadable.

"Like we said before, we have to work together," she added, feeling a bit desperate to make the point.

"I can find other office space."

"Really?"

"If that needs to happen, it can happen."

"But it's your building."

"There are other buildings."

She licked her lips. "That was at the top of my reasons why we shouldn't get involved, but it wasn't the only reason."

He gave her a serious look. "I know."

"So, for now, we should just say good night." Deciding that letting go of him would be a good step toward making that happen, she stepped back and took off his coat. She felt instantly chilled.

He put it on and then moved toward the door, pausing. "This isn't over, Kate."

"Maybe it should be."

"You said *for now,* not *forever.*"

"I probably misspoke."

He smiled. "Too late to take it back. I'll see you…soon."

As he slipped out of her apartment, she touched her fingers to her still-tingling lips, feeling mixed emotions about what she'd just called off.

It wasn't just the location of their offices that had stopped her; it was her growing feelings for Barrett. She wasn't just attracted to him physically: she was falling in love with him, and she didn't know where that could go.

It certainly couldn't go all the way, not with Barrett's bluntly stated feelings about marriage. And while it was way too early to even think about that kind of future, she wasn't sure she should start something that could never go where she would want it to go. Better to be safe than sorry. She didn't need to get her heart broken.

But as she walked into her bedroom, she was a little afraid that she'd already gotten too involved, and there might be some heartbreak headed her way.

***

Four days later, Barrett knew he was way too involved with Kate, and it wasn't because he'd seen her every day; it was because he hadn't—because every time he walked in and out of his office, his gaze went up the stairs, hoping for a glimpse of her.

When he heard her voice in the stairwell, he found himself straining to hear what she was saying, sometimes when he was in the middle of a meeting.

What the hell was wrong with him?

He hadn't been this obsessed with a woman in a long time. And this was not a woman he should be obsessed with, no matter how much he was attracted to her.

Kate would want everything from a man—she'd want love, attention—she'd want his soul.

And he couldn't imagine being able to give her anything close to that.

She knew it, too. It was why they kept coming to the brink of something more and then pulling back.

A knock came at his office door, and his heart jumped, but it wasn't Kate who stepped into his office. It was Candice Hunt.

He jumped up in surprise. "Candice, how are you?"

"Not great," she said, her eyes strained. "I'm sorry to barge in on you, Barrett. There was no one out front."

"Jackie is at lunch."

"I really need to talk to someone. Do you have a minute?"

"Of course. Sit down," he said, waving her into one of the two chairs in front of his desk. "What's going on?"

"It's the wedding."

He almost said he wasn't surprised but managed to bite back that cynical comment. "Are you and Anthony having second thoughts?"

"No. This has nothing to do with Anthony; it's my mother. We just had a meeting with Kate. I thought we were going to hire her, but right in the middle of our conversation, my mother suddenly announces that your mother suggested she talk to one more person before making the decision. Kate was really taken aback. I'd told her it was a done deal, because she came up with the perfect event, and I thought my mom would love it because we'd have the ceremony and the reception at the Conservatory of Flowers, and you know she loves gardens. I don't know what happened."

His gut tightened. "Apparently, my mother happened. And I don't think this is about your wedding at all; it's about Kate."

Candice looked confused. "Why would it be about Kate? Does she even know Kate?"

"I brought Kate to my mother's birthday party last Sunday. My mom was not happy about it. She has some crazy idea that now that Vanessa is no longer engaged, we should give it another shot."

"That is crazy. You and Vanessa were horrible together."

"I don't disagree." He paused. "Look, Candice, I don't want to tell you what to do—"

"I wish you would," she interrupted. "I would normally talk to my big brother, but David is deployed, and I certainly don't want to bother him with my trivial problems. I'd love to get your opinion."

"It's your wedding. If you want to hire Kate, hire Kate."

"But my mother is paying."

"That doesn't change the fact that it's your day, not hers. And I know your mother cares what you think."

"Not as much as she cares about what her friends think."

"You need to talk to her. You need to tell her how you feel."

"She doesn't listen."

"Make her listen. You have to fight for what you want, Candice. Otherwise, you'll regret it. But you already know that."

"I needed to hear someone else say it. Thanks," she said, wiping her watery eyes with the tissue.

"No problem."

"So, if you took Kate to your mother's party, how come I didn't see you there?"

"We left as soon as Vanessa arrived."

"Got it. I was wondering why she was there. Now I know. Well, I'll let you get back to work. Thanks for listening." Candice got to her feet and walked with him to the door. Pausing, she added, "Are you and Kate dating?"

"Uh, I wouldn't call it that."

"What would you call it?" she asked with interest.

"Honestly, I have no idea."

"I like her," Candice said. "She's a genuinely nice person. She cares about people. She's creative. She has a sense of humor. She's easy to talk to."

"She is all that," he agreed. "I like her, too."

"Are you going to do something about it?"

"Not sure yet. Now get out of here and go talk to your mother."

She gave him a kiss on the cheek. "Thanks, Barrett. You're a good substitute big brother."

"I'm happy to help."

As they moved into the outer office, the woman they'd just been talking about came through the door.

Kate stopped in surprise when she saw them.

"Candice," she said. "I thought you'd left the building with your mother."

"I stopped in to see Barrett on my way out. Kate, I want to hire you for the wedding."

"I don't think your mother feels the same way."

"I'm going to change her mind. I just wanted you to know. Don't write me off yet."

Relief ran through Kate's eyes. "I won't do that. I'd love to work on your wedding. But I just want you to make a decision that's right for you."

"Which is why I'm going to sit my mother down and have a long talk with her. I'll be in touch."

As Candice left, Kate sent him a searching look. "What just happened? Twenty minutes ago, I thought the Hunt wedding was done."

"I heard my mother stuck her nose into things."

"Yes, apparently," Kate said.

"Is that why you came down here—to see if I could get my mother out of your life?"

"No. I wasn't going to mention it," she said.

"Why not? It's my fault that Olivia is hesitating. I introduced you to my mother and put you in her line of fire."

"That's all you did—introduce me to your mother. Whatever she did is on her."

He was once again amazed by Kate's generosity. "I'll talk to her."

"Please don't speak to her on my behalf. It sounds like Candice wants to challenge her mother, so we'll just see what happens. You know, I'm beginning to think my mother, with her complete lack of interest in my life, is actually not so bad. Anyway, I came down here because I haven't seen you all week, and I wanted to know if you were still interested in going to the shower with me tomorrow night."

"I am—if the invitation is still good. After Sunday night—well, it seems like things have gotten a little complicated between us."

She stared back at him for a long moment, and for once he couldn't really tell what she was thinking. Usually, she was an open book. In fact, she often had trouble keeping her emotions off her face, but not today.

"That's true," she said slowly. "But I'd like you to come with me. I'd like you to meet my friends. Unless you think it's a bad idea, that maybe we should stop having so many dates that aren't really dates?"

He saw the worried gleam in her eyes and couldn't deny that he had his own doubts about moving forward. They were walking a fine line. Knowing what they each knew about the other's views on love and marriage, there was a good chance someone was going to get hurt. He didn't want that to be Kate. He didn't want her to feel the sting of another rejection.

On the other hand, he wasn't sure he'd be able to reject her, and what did that mean for him? Was he going to end up going down a road that had caused him so much pain once before?

"Should I take your silence for a yes?" she asked. "That you think it is a bad idea?"

"No. I think we should go to the shower together. I'd like to meet your friends."

"Especially Alex," she said lightly.

"And all the rest. What time should I pick you up? Or do you want to go from here?"

"Actually, I'll pick you up. I have to do a walk-through on a wedding venue down on the Peninsula at four and my car is going to be filled with party supplies, so it will be easier if I just come by your place around six fifteen, if that works."

"Perfect. I'll text you my address." He smiled. "It's a date."

She smiled back at him. "I keep asking myself what we're doing, Barrett."

"Let me know when you come up with an answer."

Chapter Fourteen

Kate pulled up to Barrett's house in her SUV with her trunk filled with wine, beer, food platters, and party games. Hanging out of her back seat window was a bunch of balloons. Getting out of her car, she jogged up the steps to Barrett's townhouse, which was located in the Marina, only a couple of blocks from the bay.

He opened the door with a smile, having exchanged the suit he usually wore to the office for a pair of dark jeans and a black leather jacket over a long-sleeve, dark-green sweater that matched his eyes. Her heart skipped a beat. He really was one of the most attractive men she'd ever known.

"Hi," he said.

"Are you ready?"

"Unless you want to come in?"

She wouldn't have minded seeing Barrett's home, but she was running a little late. "I think we should get going. I want to make sure I have enough time to set up."

"No problem." He pulled the door shut behind him and followed her to the car, his grin widening at the balloons.

"I know," she said, reading his expression. "It's like I'm driving a clown car, but I wanted to do balloons because they're festive and they fit the theme."

"There's a theme?" he asked, as he got into her passenger seat.

"It's a throwback shower, recreating the free, fun days of our youth. It's not going to be a traditional shower. There will be plenty of alcohol, for one. And games, but not traditional shower games. These will be fun."

"Games, huh? I think I'm going to need the alcohol. I'm beginning to wonder what I've gotten myself into," he said dryly.

"Don't worry. You're going to have a blast. The arcade alone will be worth it. I think you'll enjoy the night."

"I already am," he said, giving her a warm look that made her want to pull the car over and kiss him.

Clearing her throat, she turned her attention on the road, thinking it was good that Alex and Andrea's house was not too far away. "How was your day?" she asked, hoping some boring tale of law would slow her pulse down.

"It was good. I lost a client."

"How is that good?"

"They reconciled. Since they have two children under the age of five, I was happy to lose the business."

She gave him a quick look. "You don't sound like

a cynical divorce lawyer when you talk like that."

"Once in a while, people prove me wrong. How did your meetings go? Did you hear from Candice?"

"I did, and I didn't just get a call, I got a signed contract. She said she sat down with her mother and hashed things out. Olivia is going to take more of a back seat."

"That just means she'll be a back-seat driver," he said with a laugh.

"Probably. But I have the job, and that's exciting."

"Well, good."

"I think I owe you another thank-you. Candice told me that Olivia had changed her mind about following up with your mother's suggestion. Did you call your mom?"

"I did. I told her to stop trying to blow up Candice's wedding and your business because I don't want to get back together with Vanessa."

She glanced back at him. "That sounds very definitive."

"It was definitive. We had a long chat, and I think she finally heard me. She said she was sorry about her behavior at her party and to extend her apologies to you."

"That was nice."

"She can be reasonable on rare occasions. Anyway, I'm glad you got the job. And I think Candice has the perfect person to plan her wedding."

"She really liked your suggestion on the Conservatory of Flowers. I have you to thank for that."

"Looks like you're back in my debt," he said lightly.

"Should I ask what the payoff will be this time?"

"I'll have to think on that."

She pulled into the driveway of Andrea's house, which was a three-story mansion in Pacific Heights. "We're here. Let's check in with Andrea and then start unloading."

—➤➤◆◆◀◀—

Andrea Donovan was an attractive blonde, who gave Kate a tight hug when they greeted. Then she turned to him with a curious smile.

"Barrett Fox, Andrea Donovan," Kate introduced.

"It's nice to meet you," Andrea said. "I didn't know Kate was bringing a date. You are her date, right?"

"I believe so," he said with a grin. "I think I'm also the muscle, judging by the amount of items packed in Kate's car."

"Good. We can use some muscle. Alex had a meeting run long, so he won't be here for another twenty minutes."

"No problem. Barrett and I can handle it. I don't want you to do a thing," Kate said. "Where's Conor?"

"He's taking a late nap."

"I can't wait to see him." Kate turned to him. "Conor is Andrea's baby boy. He's adorable."

"And he'll be with our nanny most of the evening," Andrea said. "Tonight is couples' night. Liz is leaving Josh with her sister. And Jessica got a babysitter for Brandon."

"Well, you know we love the kids," Kate said.

"Yes, so do I," Andrea said with a laugh. "But it's also nice to have a break."

They spent the next fifteen minutes unloading the

car. Eventually, everything was spread across the massive counters in Andrea's gourmet kitchen. He was a little surprised there was no help around, since Andrea had mentioned a nanny, but apparently that was the extent of her staff.

"So tell me your story, Barrett," Andrea said, as she grabbed a carrot off the veggie tray and munched on it.

"I'm a lawyer," he said.

"Well, that's not much of a story."

"Andrea is a television news reporter. You might have seen her on KJTV," Kate put in.

"That's why you look familiar," he said.

"Which means questions are in my nature. How did you and Kate meet?"

"We met in the office building we are currently sharing."

"Oh, wait, you're the guy who got shot by Cupid's arrow?" Andrea asked. "The cynical, arrogant divorce attorney, who is making Kate's life a living hell?"

He glanced at Kate.

She gave him a guilty look. "I might have shared the story of how we met with Maggie and Jessica, who both have big mouths, by the way. And I didn't know you as well then." She turned to Andrea. "He's not making life a living hell. He's actually been really good to me. He took care of my grandfather after my grandmother was in an accident. He spent the night with him, so he wouldn't be alone."

"That is very nice," Andrea said, giving him a speculative look. "Sounds like Kate undersold you in the beginning."

"We didn't get off to a good start, but that's changed."

"I assume so, since you're here, and Kate knows you're going to get a grilling from just about everyone. I hope you're ready."

"I think I can handle it."

The next thirty minutes passed in a flash as Barrett took orders from Kate on what needed to go where. She was very impressive in work mode, and by the time they were finished, the house had been transformed into a party palace.

Alex arrived about three minutes before Liz and her husband Michael, who was on crutches. Michael complained that he'd made it through ten years of football without breaking a bone and now a damn bike ride had done him in. Liz told him to be happy he wasn't dead.

As the rest of the group entered the house, Barrett could barely keep them straight. Matt Kingsley, the Cougars' star, stood out, of course. His wife Julie had a sweet, gentle manner that was in opposition to Liz's more direct, outspoken nature. Although, the two women seemed to be close friends and had apparently grown up together.

Isabella was an exotically pretty woman, and her husband, Nick, clearly adored her. They shared the story Kate had told him about meeting during a tango lesson, which he thought might be one of the best first meets he'd ever heard of. Although, Jessica's story about getting stuck in her doghouse was right up there, too. Her fiancé Reid was a friendly guy, who said he wasn't too worried about all the wedding mania, because all he had to do was show up.

Then they were joined by Andrea's twin sister, Laurel, and her husband, Greg, and finally the other bride-to-be, Maggie, an attractive strawberry-blonde, and her fiancé Cole.

Everyone was friendly and welcoming. The guys were happy to get to know him. The women were a bit more wary, clearly wanting to make sure he was good for Kate. He didn't mind their protective attitudes; it told him how much they cared about their friend.

He cared about Kate, too, and he liked seeing her in her element, setting up party games, nudging the most reluctant to play, which often included him, making sure everyone was eating and drinking, and continuing to point to Maggie and Jessica and their guys as the guests of honor.

There was a lot of laughter, a lot of silliness, but it was fun—more fun than he'd had in a long time.

He'd also been invited down to the arcade and had a chance to not only play the original *Vertigo*, but the newest version that hadn't yet been released to the public.

He didn't know how long he'd been in the arcade, but Kate found him there, and promptly challenged him to a game. What she lacked in knowledge, she made up for in enthusiasm and a competitive drive that he should have expected, knowing how determined she could be. But in the end, he won, and Kate accepted her loss with good grace.

"I think with a little more practice, I could have beaten you," she told him.

"You can come over to my place any time and practice. I don't have the newest version, but I have the earlier ones."

"I'll think about it." She smiled. "You're having a good time, aren't you?"

"A great time—like everyone else. You put on an amazing party, Kate." He put his arms around her.

Her gaze widened. "Barrett, what is on your mind?"

"Kissing you."

"Here?"

"Everyone is gone, Kate. Look around. It's just you and me. And I think as the winner, I deserve a kiss."

"You should have negotiated that earlier, Counselor."

"Come on," he said, pulling her close.

She laughed, then framed his face with her hands and leaned in for a kiss.

His breath caught in his throat as their playful kiss immediately turned into a raging flood of desire. Every time he tasted her lips, he found himself wanting more. And tonight was no different.

Kate must have been feeling the same, because her lips parted, and their tongues tangled together in delicious heat.

And then someone said, "Kate."

They broke apart.

"Oops," Maggie said with a grin. "Sorry, I didn't know you'd stopped playing *Vertigo* and started playing with each other. Liz and Michael have to get home. If you want to say goodbye, now is the time."

"I do, of course," Kate said, with a flush on her cheeks, as she hurried past Maggie.

Maggie gave him a warning look. "One second, Barrett."

"What's up?"

"I just want you to know that you better do right by her. She's one in a million—make that a billion."

"I know," he said, meeting her gaze.

"Don't forget it. Or you'll have to answer to all of

us."

"Kate is lucky to have you all."

"We're lucky to have her. She always goes above and beyond, and I'm not just talking about the parties or the weddings; it's everything else. She's the first person who calls when you're sick. She'll drop everything and rush to your side if you have a flat tire or need a ride or just someone to talk to. Kate has been the glue that's held us all together. She's the one who made us into not just friends, but sisters—family. She's really important to all of us. And maybe I'm overstepping here but watching the two of you together tonight—it makes me happy and nervous. Kate doesn't give her heart easily. If she's giving it to you, I just don't want you to break it."

"I don't want that, either," he said, feeling a heavy weight in his gut. He didn't want to hurt Kate, but there was a good chance that's exactly what would happen.

"Maggie and Barrett," Andrea said, coming into the room. "Liz and Michael are waiting to say good-bye. Is everything okay?"

"Perfect. We were just chatting," Maggie said. "Shall we go?"

"After you," he told her.

⤙⤛⤜⤚

After saying good-bye to everyone and cleaning up the party supplies, Kate and Barrett got back into her car. As she started the engine, she said, "Well, what did you think? Too corny for you?"

"Just corny enough," he said lightly.

As she drove toward his house, the silence

between them lengthened, and she started to feel a little nervous. Everything had been going so well up until now. Her friends had loved Barrett. He'd fit in as if he'd known them for years, and he'd completely let go and participated in all the silly games with a willing energy. She'd been really impressed by that. There had been no sign of his cynical self.

And the kiss they'd shared after their *Vertigo* battle had been hotter than all the others.

But since then he'd been a little quiet. He also hadn't come back from the arcade right away. Neither had Maggie.

Frowning, she glanced over at him. "Barrett, did Maggie say something to you?"

"What do you mean?"

"After she caught us kissing, did she say something?"

He hesitated, then said, "She told me I better not hurt you."

"I'm sorry. She shouldn't have said that. She's assuming things that aren't true."

"I don't think she was doing that," he said quietly. "In fact, I think she was right."

She licked her lips, not liking his tone. "Right about what?"

"That you deserve someone amazing, someone who can give you the life you deserve." He turned his head, facing her with a somewhat grim look in his eyes. "I don't think that's me."

Her chest tightened as her breath got caught in her throat. She was so surprised by his words, she almost missed the stop sign. She slammed on the brakes, throwing them both a little forward.

"Sorry," she apologized again.

She drove through the intersection, then pulled over in front of his building.

"You can just block the driveway," he told her.

She did as he suggested and put the car in park, then turned toward him. "Barrett, you don't have to worry about hurting me. I'm a big girl; I can take care of myself."

He met her gaze. "You know where I stand, Kate. I don't see marriage in my future, and I know you do."

"We're a long way from talking about marriage."

"That's true, but I don't want to start something with you that can't possibly go where you want it to go."

"Don't presume to know what I want."

"Then tell me what you want," he challenged. "Tell me where I'm wrong."

She stared back at him for a long minute. *She wanted to say he was wrong, but was he? Wasn't he just echoing the doubts that had been going through her head?*

"It's really early to make long-term assumptions," she murmured.

"It is, but I like you, Kate. And I don't want to hurt you. I want you to have everything you want, and I know that's marriage and family. You want the big romance, the life-or-death love affair, the magnificent gesture, and you should have all of that. But for me, I don't think I want to go down that road again. I'm not cut out to be a husband and probably not a father. Maybe it would be better if we stop right where we are. We'll be office friends."

"Office friends, huh?"

"I'll move out as soon as I can find some other space."

She felt a heaviness in her heart, but it was difficult to fight back against the truth. She did want a happily ever after. She wanted a family, a husband, a father for whatever children she would have. She deserved that. She'd grown up in a broken home, and no matter how great her grandparents had been, they still hadn't been her parents. She wanted to put together a traditional family. She wanted to marry someone forever.

Maybe it was all a pipe dream. Perhaps they were acting prematurely. No one could predict the future. But she couldn't go into a relationship, knowing there was no hope of getting what she wanted.

"You don't have to move," she said. "If you want this to be over, then it's over."

"Just like that."

"Just like that," she echoed. "I'm not going to make a scene."

"Okay," he said, looking a little unsure now that she'd agreed with him.

"But I think you're wrong, Barrett. I think you could be an amazing husband and father. And I'm a little sad that you can't see that, that you can't allow yourself to take another chance. But maybe the right woman would make you feel differently."

"This isn't about you; it's about me."

"It's about both of us. You should go, Barrett." She really needed him to get out of the car before she broke down. Already, she could feel the emotions rising within her. She was sad and angry and disappointed. But she needed to keep it together.

"All right. Good night, Kate," he said, a somber note in his voice. He gave her one last, searching look and then got out of the car.

She took off as soon as the door closed, needing to put some distance between them before the tears started to fall.

Chapter Fifteen

What the hell had he done? Barrett wondered almost three weeks later when the reality of not seeing Kate had sunk all the way in. It wasn't just that he hadn't seen her outside of work; he hadn't even caught a glimpse of her going in and out of the building. And he didn't like it.

He should like it.

He should be happy she'd agreed to stop before things got more complicated between them, before they got more involved, before there was no hope of avoiding a painful end.

But this felt painful, too.

Sitting back in his office chair, he stretched his arms over his head, then glanced at his watch. It was almost four. He had no more clients coming in today and tomorrow was Friday. He couldn't wait for the work week to be over. Although, the looming weekend didn't make him feel any better. He was dreading the empty days, when he would have too much time to think and to feel.

His entire life seemed to be cloudy and gray. And it didn't take a rocket scientist to figure out why. It was Kate.

She'd brought color and laughter, fun and hope back into his life. She'd made him want more than he'd wanted in a long time. He missed talking to her. He missed seeing her smile. He missed hearing her crazy stories. He missed kissing her.

A knock came at his door, and he straightened in surprise. Jackie had left an hour earlier, after his last client. "Come in," he said.

"Hi, Barrett." Maggie walked in the door, giving him a tentative smile.

He got to his feet. "Maggie. Are you looking for Kate?"

"No. I just saw her. She's upstairs in her office, working away on the final details for our wedding this Saturday. She's doing what she does, trying not to look completely miserable."

He didn't know what to say to that. Fortunately, Maggie didn't seem to expect an answer.

"Kate told me that the two of you aren't seeing each other anymore and that it happened the night of the shower. I think I'm partly responsible. When I said what I said to you, I was sort of joking."

"You were not joking; you were serious. You were looking out for Kate."

"Okay, I was, but I stuck my nose where it didn't belong. It wasn't my business. I apologized to Kate, and I also wanted to tell you I'm sorry. What you and Kate do is your own business. And I should have kept my mouth shut."

"You only reminded me what was at stake. And I

don't want to hurt Kate."

"But she's already hurting. I probably shouldn't tell you that, but it's true. Anyway, I just thought you should know." She turned and walked toward the door, then paused. "Kate is an amazing person. I hope you realize just what you're missing out on." She blew out a breath. "Okay, now I'm done."

As she left his office, he sank back into his chair, thinking about what she'd said.

Maggie was wrong.

He knew exactly what he was missing out on; he just didn't know what to do about it.

⸻

Maggie and Jessica's Valentine's Day wedding went off without a hitch—two beautiful brides and their handsome grooms exchanging their vows in a beautiful church in the Presidio.

The reception at what had once been the Officer's Club was also going well. As Kate wandered through the room, smiling at her friends, checking on details, she felt a little teary-eyed.

Maggie and Jessica were the last of her close circle of friends to get married. They'd had so much fun the past couple of years, sending everyone off to their future in grand style.

And this was the last wedding.

Well, she supposed one day she'd have a wedding—*maybe*.

Or maybe her destiny was to put everyone else together.

She sighed at that depressing thought.

"Kate," Jessica said, striding toward her in her

beautiful dress. "Thank you again. Everything has been perfect."

"The way it should be," she declared.

Jessica's gaze softened. "I just wish you were happier."

"Me? I'm fine. I'm very happy. All the work is done. Now it's just fun."

They'd had a morning wedding, because Maggie and Cole were taking a late-night flight to London to start their European honeymoon. It was almost five now, and the band would be stopping soon. Then the brides and their grooms would make their exit.

"Have you thought about talking to Barrett?" Jessica asked.

"Look, I know you're all worried about me, but you don't have to be. I'll get over Barrett. I have to," she said a little desperately. It would help if she could stop thinking about him for more than five minutes, but so far that hadn't happened. He'd been on her mind constantly. She'd tried to stay out of the office as much as possible, so much even Shari had started to worry about her.

"Instead of getting over him, why don't you talk to him?" Jessica suggested.

"Because we said all there was to say."

"Didn't that conversation last like five minutes?" Jessica challenged.

"I really need to stop telling all of you every detail of my life," she grumbled.

"I'm just saying, maybe a longer discussion is in order."

"He never wants to get married, Jessica, and I'm a wedding planner. He's a cynic. I'm a romantic. It won't work."

"I actually understand the way he feels, Kate. I went through a lot of the same emotions when I started falling for Reid. I didn't think I ever wanted to get married after my disaster of a first marriage."

"But you got married the first time because you were pregnant; that was different. Barrett married someone he thought he loved at the time, and it crashed and burned."

"Which is why he's afraid to go down the aisle again. I almost bailed on Reid for the same reason— fear. But Reid wouldn't let me. He made me realize that love was worth the risk of more pain. Maybe you need to remind Barrett of that."

"I can't talk him into changing his mind. He has to do that on his own. But I don't think that will happen. He's pretty stubborn."

Jessica smiled. "You can be stubborn, too, Kate. And it's not like you to give up. Are you really going to let this great guy walk away without a fight?"

"I don't want to, but...maybe I'm a little scared, too. Maybe it's easier this way."

"Since when do you take the easy way out?"

"Since now."

"Kate," Jessica said.

"I'll think about it. But not today. It's almost time for you and Maggie to change and say your good-byes." She paused, turning her head at the sound of loud voices near the front door.

"Kate," Maggie called from the doorway. "You have to see this."

See what? she wondered, her gaze narrowing as guests started streaming outside.

Liz ran over to her and grabbed her hand, her eyes sparkling. "Come outside."

"What's going on?"

"You have to see it to believe it," Liz told her, dragging her out to the front steps.

There was a loud buzz of a very low-flying plane. She looked up at the sky, shocked to see her name written in the sky, followed by the words *I Love You*.

"I don't understand," she muttered.

"It's Barrett," Maggie said, pointing to the sky where the letter B had just formed.

"Why would he do this?" she asked in confusion. "We're not together."

"But I want us to be." Barrett's voice rang out behind her, and she whirled around.

Barrett was standing on the steps, dressed in the same black suit he'd worn the first night she'd met him. In his hand was an arrow.

"Remember when this thing hit me?" he asked.

She shook her head in bemusement.

"You don't remember?" he asked in surprise.

"I remember, but I don't understand how you have it. I cleaned up the broken statue."

"Somehow this arrow ended up in my pocket." He stepped forward as her friends fell back in an arc behind her.

He took her hands as he gazed at her with beautiful green eyes that sparkled in the sunlight. "When Cupid shot his arrow at me, I thought I was invincible, that no one could pierce the wall I'd built around my heart. But that wasn't true. You barreled right through it." He let that sink in, then added, "I'm an idiot, Kate. I never should have called things off with you. You're the most amazing woman I've ever met, and I'm in love with you."

It was almost impossible to believe the words

coming out of Barrett's mouth. "You—are you sure?"

"Positive. I knew the first moment I met you that you were going to complicate my life. But I didn't know how much I would care about you. I haven't been able to stop thinking about you. The last few weeks I've found myself listening for the sound of your footsteps upstairs, the faint echo of a laugh coming down the stairwell."

"I've done the same," she confessed. "I actually worked from home the other day, because I wasn't getting anything done. But how we feel doesn't change the fact that we don't want the same things."

"I've been hanging on to my rigid viewpoints for far too long. The truth is, I want you, Kate. And I want to see where all this goes."

"Even if it goes toward a church and a reception?"

He smiled with complete candor in his gaze. "Even then. I'm not ruling anything out."

"Seriously? Why the change of heart?"

"You're the reason. You told me before that when I met the right person, I'd want it all, and I do. I want it with you. I want to make you happy."

"I want to make you happy, too. I don't want to force anything on you."

"You're not. This is my choice. Frankly, I don't know why I took so long to get here."

"Well, we don't have to rush into anything. We can take our time. Really get to know each other."

"As long as we're taking our time together, I'm good," he told her. "But I want you to know that I'm willing to go the distance."

"I can't believe you hired a plane to write our names in the sky."

He smiled down at her. "You said something once about wanting a man who's willing to make a magnificent gesture of love. I'm hoping this counts."

"It does. It really does," she said, unbelievable happiness running through her.

"But I didn't just do this for you, Kate—I did it for me. I needed to tell not just you but also the world how I feel. I needed to stop hiding and declare myself. And if one of us gets hurt, well, at least we won't have to wonder *what if.*"

"I agree. I've been scared, too. But whatever happens, I'd rather be with you for as long as it works than be without because I'm afraid. My grandparents have always told me that love is worth the risk."

"Then we're finally on the same page."

"Kiss him already," Maggie called out, echoed by the other bridesmaids.

He grinned. "I think the crowd has spoken."

She wrapped her arms around his neck and lifted her mouth to his, feeling a rush of joy and pleasure as their lips met.

And then there was a round of applause.

She pulled away with a somewhat embarrassed smile. "I'm sorry, Maggie and Jessica. This is supposed to be your day."

The two brides came forward and hugged her.

"You made our day," Maggie said.

Jessica nodded. "I couldn't be happier for you, Kate."

"Looks like we have one more wedding," Andrea said.

"Hold on," she protested. "Barrett and I just agreed to see where things go."

"You know where they're going to go," Isabella

said with a sweet, knowing smile.

"She's right," Julie put in. "You've always told us to trust our instincts. Now you need to do the same."

"And we'll be your bridesmaids," Laurel said.

"But you can't plan your own wedding, can you?" Liz asked.

She put up a hand. "Everyone needs to slow down. Let's finish this wedding, before we start worrying about another. The band is playing for another…ten minutes," she said, checking her watch. "I think we should all have one more dance."

As the crowd wandered back into the building, she turned back to Barrett. "Want to dance with me?"

"For the rest of my life," he promised, taking her hand in his. "I want us to be like your grandparents."

"I want that, too," she whispered, kissing him again. "Happy Valentine's Day."

Epilogue

$\rightarrow\!\!\gg\!\!\ll\!\!\leftarrow$

Sixteen months later...

Barrett met his brother's gaze in the mirror, and he was reminded of when they'd done this before. But this time they weren't wearing tuxedos, just dark-gray suits. And this time there was only a crowd of fifty or so waiting in a very small church in the Napa Valley, that would be packed to the rafters, if all fifty showed up. After that, they'd be heading down the street to the inn run by Maggie and Cole, where a summer garden and beautiful patio area were set up for a party that would last well past midnight.

This time he was marrying the right woman—he was marrying Kate.

"Ready?" Matt asked, a slightly nervous edge in his voice. "No second thoughts, right?"

"Don't worry. I'm not going to be a runaway groom," he joked.

"Good to know. I'd have to come after you and

kick your ass, because you will never find anyone better for you than Kate."

He turned to face his brother. "I knew that the first day I met her. But the last year and a half has made me realize how close I came to missing out on someone very special, just because I was too scared to fail again."

"You're not going to fail—not this time."

"I'm not even worried about it. I love Kate, and I can't wait to marry her, because I know what we're both looking forward to the most is the actual marriage."

Matt smiled and gave a nod. "You've definitely changed since you met Kate. You're more relaxed, more yourself. You've softened. You're fun again."

"Hard not to have fun when I'm with Kate and her friends."

"She does have a good group of female friends, and the guys are great, too. We had a hell of a bachelor party. And I still can't believe we were hanging out with Alexander Donovan, the creator of *Vertigo*."

"One of these days, I'll have to get you into the private arcade at his house. You will never want to leave."

"Sounds like a plan, but for now, I think we should get you married."

"Are our parents here?"

"Mom and James are in the first row, along with Aunt Joan and Uncle Harry and their two kids. Dad and Tanya are at the end of that row, so hopefully our parents have enough buffers between them. They won't actually have to talk to each other."

"Well, frankly, I don't care what they do. The

only person I want to be happy today is Kate."

"I like the sound of that," a man said from the doorway.

Barrett turned to see Kate's grandfather come into the room. His blue eyes were bright and smiling with happiness. "Hello, Lance."

The older man shook his hand and then nodded to his brother. "Matt—good to see you."

"You, too. Is your beautiful bride with you?"

"Bess is headed in to see Kate to wish her well. Not that either of you need luck. You've got love on your side. I've seen it grow every day."

"Sometimes I can hardly believe how much I love her," he said. "And I hope you know that you and Bess are an inspiration to both Kate and me."

"I'm glad. I knew you were the one when I showed you her ballet videos and you watched every minute without even checking your watch."

"It took me awhile to admit it, but I fell for her fast."

"She fell just as quickly. I think the two of you are going to make it. You're a lot like Bess and me. You don't just love each other, you laugh together."

"Is that the secret?" Matt asked. "For a long, happy marriage?"

"It's one of them."

"What are the others?" Barrett asked.

"Well, practically speaking, you should always get your wife a birthday present, even if she says she doesn't want one, always tell her she looks good, and if she asks you to pick an outfit, pick one, otherwise, she'll think you don't care. And be forgiving. Neither of you are perfect. But it's all the imperfections that make life the most interesting."

"Noted," he said with a smile. "I think I can do all that."

"You can and you will. Or I'll have something to say about it."

"Got it," he said.

"I'll see you in the church."

As Lance left, Matt smiled at him. "I might have to take some of Lance's advice, too."

"You and Amy?" he asked with a quirk of his brow.

"Getting close," Matt replied. "But let's get you married first."

———※※———

"You look beautiful, honey," her grandmother told her, as she stepped into the dressing room.

Her friends had all moved into the outer hall to give them a few moments of privacy.

"Thanks, Grandma," she said, giving her a kiss on the cheek.

"Your mother is in the church. She said she'd talk to you after."

"That's fine. You're the one who has been the real mother to me all these years, the one who helped me plan this wedding, the one who brought me up to be the best person I can be. I'm so grateful, Grandma."

Her grandmother's eyes blurred with tears. "Oh, Katie, you're going to make me cry and ruin my makeup."

"I just want you to know how much I love you."

"I love you, too. And I love Barrett. He's a good man and he's the right man for you. He'll support you, but he'll also encourage you to be all you can be. And you'll do the same for him."

She and Barrett had spent a lot of time with her grandparents in the past year and a half, and she'd been pleased at how well they'd all gotten along.

"Anyway, I'll let you spend the last few minutes with your bridesmaids," her grandmother said. "I'll see you after the ceremony."

"Thanks."

As her grandmother left, her bridesmaids came into the room.

As she looked at the group of her very best friends, the women who would stand by her side not just today but always, she felt incredibly blessed. Maybe her parents had been next to worthless, but she had wonderful grandparents, great friends, and a loving man she would soon call her husband. She was incredibly lucky.

"Okay, usually you do the champagne, but I am handling it today," Maggie said, passing out champagne glasses to everyone.

"You all look beautiful," she said.

She'd put her bridesmaids in dark-blue cocktail dresses that they could definitely wear again, while she'd chosen a beautiful fitted gown with hand-placed beads, a plunging neckline and an open back. It was her biggest splurge. The rest of her wedding was actually quite modest by most standards, and that wasn't because Barrett had wanted things simple. He'd given her free rein to plan everything, but she'd found after planning so many over-the-top weddings that what she wanted for herself was something small and intimate.

"So do you, Kate," Jessica said. "Maybe the most beautiful bride of all."

"Well, I'm the last one anyway," she said with a laugh. "What should we toast to?"

"Let's toast to us," Andrea said. "To eight friends who came together in the first year of college, who navigated the school years with the help of each other and grew up to be amazing women. To Laurel, who started us off on our bridesmaid journey. To Liz, who found love with her first crush and to Julie, who got over her hatred of baseball players to find the love of her life. To Maggie, who took a walk on the wild side with a rebel biker, who turned out to be so much more. To Isabella, who danced her way into Nicholas's heart and to Jessica, who got it right the second time around after getting stuck in a doghouse." Andrea paused, looking at her with a smile. "Finally, to Kate, who helped get us all down the aisle and now it's her turn."

"And to you, Andrea," Kate put in. "Who put love before career to marry an incredible man and who hosts all of our amazing parties."

"To us," Andrea said, as they lifted their glasses and then clinked them against each other.

Kate took a sip of champagne and then set down her glass. She took one last look in the mirror, barely recognizing her reflection. Her blue eyes were lit up, and her skin was glowing. She looked like a woman in love, and that's exactly what she was.

"I'm ready," she said.

Maggie gave her a smile. "Then let's get you married."

Barrett had been nervous the first time he'd stood

at the altar, but tonight he felt nothing but complete and utter calm as Kate followed her bridesmaids down the aisle.

She'd opted to walk alone. She wanted to give herself to him. And he wanted to give himself to her. They were surrounded by family and friends, but this moment was theirs.

As she joined him in front of the altar, she gave him a smile that was filled with love. His heart twisted in his chest. He felt almost knocked out by the look in her eyes and by the feelings running through him.

He had not felt like this before. He had not felt so absolutely certain of what they were doing.

The minister began the ceremony, making it personal, and even a little amusing. He related the story of their first meeting, relating it to divine intervention or perhaps even Cupid.

And maybe the minister was right, because that arrow had struck him right before he'd met Kate. Maybe that's exactly what he'd needed to get him out of the rut he'd been in.

They exchanged vows that were also unique to them and ended the ceremony with a long, tender kiss that was filled with their promises to each other.

They walked down the aisle to applause from their guests, and once they reached the outside steps, he pulled her into his arms and gave her another kiss.

"There will be time for that later," Maggie chided as the bridesmaids and ushers surrounded them.

"Picture time," Liz declared.

"Let's get everyone in the photos," Kate said, as the group gathered on the steps. "Including all the kids."

Barrett laughed as Isabella's new baby girl, who

was barely two months old, was placed in her arms, while Liz, Andrea and Julie wrangled in their toddlers and Jessica and her budding preteen huddled with Reid. He hadn't just gained a wife, he'd gained a group of friends. He'd gained a family. But he didn't want just this family; he wanted the one he would have with Kate.

He looked down at his beautiful wife. "Happy?"

"More than I could have ever imagined. And last single girl standing no more," she murmured with a smile. "You were worth the wait, Barrett."

"I agree. We're going to make it, Kate. At least fifty or sixty years."

"Or forever," she said.

"I just hope that's long enough."

She took his hand, and then they turned and smiled for the camera.

THE END

Get the whole series!

About The Author

Barbara Freethy is a #1 New
York Times Bestselling Author of 66
novels ranging from contemporary
romance to romantic suspense and
women's fiction. Traditionally
published for many years, Barbara
opened her own publishing company
in 2011 and has since sold over 7
million books! Twenty of her titles
have appeared on the New York
Times and USA Today Bestseller Lists.

Known for her emotional and compelling stories of love,
family, mystery and romance, Barbara enjoys writing about
ordinary people caught up in extraordinary adventures.
Barbara's books have won numerous awards. She is a six-time
finalist for the RITA for best contemporary romance from
Romance Writers of America and a two-time winner for
DANIEL'S GIFT and THE WAY BACK HOME.

Barbara has lived all over the state of California and
currently resides in Northern California where she draws much
of her inspiration from the beautiful bay area.

For a complete listing of books, as well as excerpts and
contests, and to connect with Barbara:

Visit Barbara's Website:
www.barbarafreethy.com

Join Barbara on Facebook:
www.facebook.com/barbarafreethybooks

Follow Barbara on Twitter:
www.twitter.com/barbarafreethy